Tin House

MAGAZINE

Volume 20, Number 3

"In an age of madness, to expect to be untouched by madness is a form of madness. But the pursuit of sanity can be a form of madness, too."

—SAUL BELLOW

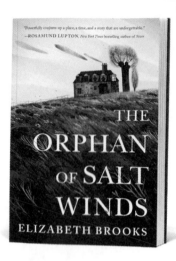

THE ORPHAN OF SALT WINDS

a novel by Elizabeth Brooks

For fans of Eowyn Ivey, Rose Tremaine, and Kate Atkinson, *The Orphan of Salt Winds* is a bewitching debut about the secrets that haunt us.

"A beautifully written, atmospheric novel—reminiscent of *Jane Eyre* with its wild, bleak setting and houseful of mysteries. Bewitching and haunting."

—EOWYN IVEY, author of *Snow Child*

The Orphan of Salt Winds is an atmospheric, ...tifully paced novel about sacrifice, the urge ...long, and revenge. It is full of well-drawn ...acters I loved to hate, and those I didn't ... let go, even after I closed the last page."

...AIRE FULLER, author of *Bitter Orange*

MAGICAL NEGRO

poetry by Morgan Parker

A profound and deceptively funny exploration of Black American womanhood.

"The firebrand behind *There Are More Beautiful Things Than Beyoncé* pens another lay-it-all-on-the-line volume of scorching verse."

—*O, the Oprah Magazine*

"If you're anxious for your snug perspective to be rattled and ripped asunder, for the predictable landscape you stroll to become all but unrecognizable, for things you thought you knew to slap you into another consciousness—brethren, have I got the book for you. Bey's bestie continues her reign with this restless, fierce, and insanely inventive way of walking through the world. Once again, children—ignore Ms. Parker at your peril."

—PATRICIA SMITH, author of *Incendiary Art*

Available Now   **Available Now**

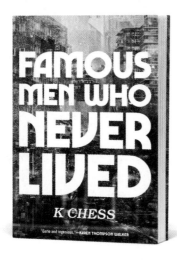

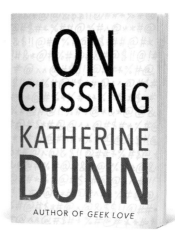

FAMOUS MEN WHO NEVER LIVED
a novel by K Chess

For readers of *Station Eleven* and
Exit West, *Famous Men Who Never Lived*
explores the effect of displacement on our
identities, the communities that come
together through circumstance, and
the power of art to save us.

"Eerie and ingenious . . . This inventive book
does what only fiction can do: describes an
impossible world in order to more clearly
show us our own."

—KAREN THOMPSON WALKER,
author of *The Dreamers*

"A fascinating novel: complex,
uncanny, powerful."

—DANA SPIOTTA,
author of *Innocents and Others*

ON CUSSING
by Katherine Dunn

Cult hero and National Book Award
finalist Katherine Dunn teaches us how to
curse with maximum effect.

"[Dunn's prose is] a pyrotechnic medium
so far removed from our workaday speech that
it feels unfair and inaccurate to call that
fire-language 'English.'"

—KAREN RUSSELL, in *Wired*

"Dunn grafted vaudeville vernacular
onto a cool classicism, a prose style at once
effortless and extravagant."

—*The Atlantic*

Available March 5, 2019

Available March 26, 2019

GIVE A LIT.
Shop independent.

POWELL'S
CITY of BOOKS | VISIT US AT POWELLS.COM

Tin House
MAGAZINE

EDITOR IN CHIEF / PUBLISHER
Win McCormack

EDITOR Rob Spillman
DEPUTY PUBLISHER Holly MacArthur
ART DIRECTOR Diane Chonette
MANAGING EDITOR Cheston Knapp
EXECUTIVE EDITOR Michelle Wildgen
SENIOR EDITOR Emma Komlos-Hrobsky
EDITOR-AT-LARGE Elissa Schappell
ASSOCIATE EDITOR Thomas Ross
POETRY EDITOR Camille T. Dungy
SENIOR DESIGNER Jakob Vala
PARIS EDITOR Heather Hartley
COPY EDITOR Meg Storey

CONTRIBUTING EDITORS: Dorothy Allison, Steve Almond, Aimee Bender, Charles D'Ambrosio, Natalie Diaz, Anthony Doerr, Nick Flynn, Matthea Harvey, Jeanne McCulloch, Rick Moody, Maggie Nelson, Whitney Otto, D. A. Powell, Jon Raymond, Helen Schulman, Jim Shepard, Karen Shepard

INTERNS: Margaret Cassinelli, Elena Ender, Carolyn Grigar, Nike Laskaris, Morgan O'Sullivan, Kelsey Stoneberger

READERS: Leslie Marie Aguilar, William Clifford, April Darcy, Selin Gökçesu, Todd Gray, Lisa Grgas, Carol Keeley, Louise Wareham Leonard, Su-Yee Lin, Maria Lioutaia, Alyssa Persons, Sean Quinn, Lauren Roberts, Gordon Smith, Jennifer Taylor, J. R. Toriseva, Charlotte Wyatt

Tin House Magazine (ISSN 1541-521X) is published quarterly by McCormack Communications LLC, 2601 Northwest Thurman Street, Portland, OR 97210. Vol. 20, No. 3, Spring 2019. Printed by Kingery Printing. Send submissions (with SASE) to Tin House, P.O. Box 10500, Portland, OR 97296-0500. ©2019 McCormack Communications LLC. All rights reserved. No part of this publication may be reproduced, stored in a retrieval system, or transmitted in any form or by any means, electronic, mechanical, photocopying, recording, or otherwise, without the prior written permission of McCormack Communications LLC. Visit our Web site at **www.tinhouse.com**.

Basic subscription price: one year, $50.00. For subscription requests, write to P.O. Box 469049, Escondido, CA 92046-9049, or e-mail tinhouse@pcspublink.com, or call 1-800-786-3424. Circulation management by Circulation Specialists, Inc.

Periodicals postage paid at Portland, OR 97210 and additional mailing offices.

Postmaster: Send address changes to Tin House Magazine, P.O. Box 469049, Escondido, CA 92046-9049.

Newsstand distribution through Disticor Magazine Distribution Services (disticor.com). If you are a retailer and would like to order Tin House, call 905-619-6565, fax 905-619-2903, or e-mail Melanie Raucci at mraucci@disticor.com. For trade copies, contact W. W. Norton & Company at 800-233-4830.

In the cycle of life spring is the season of rebirth. As the long dark and cold days of winter fade, the world reawakens. Leaves burst forth and flowers riot into blossom; seeds sown in fall begin to bear fruit. The future is ripe with endless possibilities. Even so, in this moment of supreme aliveness, we can't help but remember the past, what has been lost, and yet never goes away.

Memory is like that. No matter how deep they're buried, or how long they've lain dormant, memories inevitably force their way back up to the surface of our consciousness. Only they aren't exactly the same; the years have altered them, and the way we live with them, and even the painful memories can be tinged with nostalgia.

Cicero famously said, "Sweet is the memory of past troubles." This bittersweet interplay that exists between remembered pain and joy is fertile ground for several of our authors. In "Flycatcher," Aleksandar Hemon teases apart the subtle social navigations teenagers make, willingly or unwillingly, to distinguish themselves, and how these choices reverberate through time and memory. In Rachel Eliza Griffiths's poem "Good Mother," she writes, "We held on & praised the nameless thing /that makes us what we think we aren't strong enough /to know." The urge to stop time and with it a collective feeling, animates Maria Lioutaia's story "Preservation," in which Lenin's preserved body begins to disintegrate and the mausoleum's director turns to the living in order to suspend the inevitable.

As when you experience spring, when you read great writing you can feel as if there are powerful, unseen forces just below the surface. You can feel their pull, and you probably have a very strong sense of what they look and feel like. Sometimes it helps to have someone help you see and name them. Let our writers be your guide in this time of renewal and regeneration. Happy, or at least thought-provoking, spring.

CONTENTS

ISSUE #79 / SPRING FLING

Fiction

Poetry

FICTION

What You Seek is Seeking You

Jo Ann Beard

"YOU GOTTA TAKE THE DOG," NATHAN INSISTED, OVER THE phone. "Don't you remember how much you love the dog?"

"I admired the dog," Stephen said. "Totally different thing."

Aiko had once caught a squirrel and then let it go in a mind-blowing act of canine chivalry. Stephen, visiting, had seen the whole thing from his brother's deck: the dog ambling through the garden, her stomach swinging from side to side, sniffing thoughtfully at clumps of flowers and freshening up her scent trail. Across the yard a squirrel paused upside down at the base of a tree, its tail pulsing. Suddenly, the dog made her move, the squirrel twisted feverishly back and forth and then gave up, hanging limply from Aiko's mouth, eyes bright, waiting for what would come next.

"I never told you this before," Stephen said, "but Melissa told her to kill it. She threw open the bedroom window and goes, *Fucking kill it you mutt*." Melissa was Nathan's wife, tall and erratic, an elementary school teacher who was constantly saying and doing things you didn't want to associate with children.

"Oh my God!" Nathan murmured, appalled. "Isn't that *exactly* what I've been saying?"

Stephen knew where this was going. He was either going to have to agree to take their dog or he was going to have to listen to Nathan's circuitous explanation once again about why he had been having sex with the woman who did their taxes.

"See, Melissa could even make a *dog* go against its own nature! I'm telling you, there's something about her that makes you just want to do the opposite of what she tells you." Nathan listened for a moment to the noncommittal sound of his brother paying no attention, the intermittent crumple of a newspaper. "You just have to disagree with somebody like that, right? Don't you?" Nothing. "*Fucking kill it you mutt*, and the dog drops the squirrel. I mean,

JO ANN BEARD

you basically have to drop the squirrel; it's the only reasonable response. Let me ask you," he said, as though this was a new thought, one that had just come to him. "Can you believe I stayed married to her for almost four years?"

"Who, the dog?"

"What?"

"You were talking about the dog, and then you said, 'Can you believe I stayed married to her for almost four years?'"

"What the fuck are you talking about?" Nathan said, peering into the fridge. He was going to make himself some eggs. Fuck the way he'd been living, Pop-Tarts thirty times a day. Fuck Melissa and fuck Renee, too, for that matter, signing up for an online dating service; him having to run across her self-satisfied face on his computer screen at three o'clock in the morning.

"You were talking about the dog, and then you said, 'Can you believe . . .'"

"Could you shut up? You got any awareness of how backward you are? I mean, you're my brother but you can't even follow a simple conversation." The last egg in the carton had something dark green smeared across the shell. "This is just great," Nathan cried. The pan clattered in Stephen's ear. Stephen turned the page of his newspaper. War, war, and more war. He heard the sound of Pop-Tarts being fed into the toaster.

"How many of those do you eat a day?" he asked.

"Why don't you come out here and cook for me, you ignorant fucking nerd?" Nathan shouted into the phone, so loudly that Stephen shrieked in response. It felt like someone had stuck a tuning fork directly into his ear canal.

"Nice high-pitched scream," Nathan said, laughing meanly.

When the dog had set the squirrel down on the grass it flipped over and then vanished; a microsecond later it stared down, panting, from a high branch.

"All right," Stephen said. "Send her."

So Nathan put Aiko on a flight in San Francisco, and she arrived in Ithaca eight hours later (six hours after the tranquilizer wore off), foam-flecked and trembling. Stephen, who was running about a half hour late, found her in the baggage claim area, the crate haphazardly dumped into a corner, so

> Fuck the way he'd been living, Pop-Tarts thirty times a day.

that in the echoing swirl of airport bustle, she could see only a scuffed wall. He turned the crate around with his foot and bent down to take a look. There was a heavyset yellow dog, peering out with a look of desperate, studied blankness on her broad face.

She spent her days in Stephen's backyard, standing on top of the picnic table barking ceaselessly at the gray Ithaca sky, or doing demolition work on his lawn, digging not holes but salad-bowl-sized depressions every few feet, and pulling down the trumpet vines that clung to the tall wooden fence. She would tug on them until they were stretched across the grass in long strands, their narrow purple flowers collapsing like wet crepe paper. Sometimes she napped in the poppy bed for an hour or so, sprawled on her back with her pale belly exposed, large dirty paws retracted against her chest, stout body framed by the delicate fronds smashed flat beneath her.

"We do *not* do that," Stephen would tell her firmly, pointing to the ankle-turning holes, the trampled flower beds, the quarter-inch-deep toenail grooves in his back door. "*Ever*. Not."

> "So what, you're helping someone out for once," she replied briskly.

She whimpered in agreement and bolted in a fevered, dirt-churning circle, barking hoarsely into the evening air. As Stephen crouched to pet her, she raked her front paw across his face.

Since Nathan had stopped taking his calls, he complained instead to his mother. "My yard is now toast," he said into her answering machine.

She picked up while he was still speaking.

"So what, you're helping someone out for once," she replied briskly. "What's a yard? Is there anything more meaningless?"

This to a plant biologist, the son who worshipped moss. Next to his bed, right now, was a catalog of nothing but varieties of fern. Every luminous green imaginable, every kind of intricate fringe.

"Thanks for your understanding," he said.

"Thank *you*, Stephen, for assisting your brother," she replied pleasantly. "If Nathan can mend his situation, then he must do so; if not, he'll move ahead." She paused, pointedly, and then went on. "Perhaps you'll learn something by being involved with this, about how to conduct a successful relationship."

"Say *what?*" Stephen asked.

"You heard me," she said. "And we're not going to belabor it."

His mother, Eleanor Klein, was an elderly and formidable pediatrician who still saw patients three days a week. She also managed Stephen's father, an Alzheimered scientist who spent those same three days in his office at UC Berkeley, worrying the pens in his penholder and asking the secretaries staticky questions over speakerphone.

Eleanor packed him a lunch, spoke forthrightly to one of his colleagues about accompanying him to the washroom—if he went by himself, he tended to get stuck inside the repeating pattern of identical stalls—then drove to the clinic, where for seven or so hours mothers (and sometimes fathers) would place their babies on the examining table and tell her stories of their charm and precociousness.

"Yes, well," she would reply. "We expect that at this age."

The information Stephen's father requested of the secretaries was highly specific but nonsensical, like the quasi-scientific talk in science fiction movies. His voice toggled in and out as he fiddled with the phone, making him seem more and more like an astronaut lost forever in outer space.

"I'm not sure, Morrie, but shall I check for you?" one of the secretaries would call out from her side of the transmission.

"Yes, please do, and *bring* me the answer, don't page me," he would order them.

"And where will you be?" Said a little meanly, perhaps, because although he'd had Alzheimer's for the last three years, he'd been demanding for at least thirty.

He would look around, swiveling in his chair. Wall, window, picture, papers.

"I don't know," he would say.

The Kleins had always been high achievers. The parents had both studied to become doctors and both were subjected to the quota system, allowed to succeed only if others of their brethren didn't. In Morris's case, it was an accepted practice—in Canada, Jews had to get better scores than everyone else in order to qualify for a higher education, so Morris shrugged and did what they asked, ranking just above his peers, WASPs and Jews and whatever else they threw at him. He went on, and then on again, to become a doctor of science, a botanist who made a name for himself in the delicate, knife-petaled world of lilies.

Eleanor, educated in the States, was subjected to equal and alternating doses of contempt and admiration. She ignored both, for years methodically chiseling her way through the granite ceiling until she found herself in the bracing, ammonia-scented air of pediatric medicine. She did a residency in Africa, and met her husband there, he of the pith helmet and wild eyebrows. It was like a waking dream—the blue cinder-block clinic, her fingers pressing a silver disk against narrow brown backs, the glaring sunlight, the feverish, ecstatic nights.

When Stephen was a child, they moved from Canada so that his father could take a job as a university professor and researcher in Champaign-Urbana, Illinois. In every direction, deserted roads and long green corridors of corn. Riding in the back seat in the summertime, dazed by hot wind, Stephen and Nathan would stare out their respective windows, taking in dizzying insubstantial glimpses down each row until they were carsick.

Stephen was the smartest kid in his class, always, and the strangest. He was a nerd, with a high nasal voice and fine black hair floating above his scalp, long gibbony arms that were always in the air, the left one resting on its elbow, propping up the right one during the lengthy period that the teacher stared around at the other students, waiting.

"I don't want another answer from Stephen," she would say to them ten times a day, and he'd reluctantly put the arm down. Another ten times, though, she'd have to give up, because even with the bar lowered, her students would stare at her, waiting for her to call on the Jew and get it over with.

In a precise and scathing voice she'd address Stephen without looking at him. "I guess you're going to have to help us out."

With that, he'd deliver the answer in an offhand staccato style.

Walking home at the end of the day, he was routinely attacked and pummeled by all manner of schoolchildren. His own classmates, weighty midwestern kids, thuggy older boys, giant girls with red fists. He had two semi-friends, wispy kids nobody else liked, who would whale on him as well, just for the sake of it, twisting his arms, kicking him in the shinbones, pulling on his thin foamy hair until he was flailing and grunting. But even as this was occurring—as they stormed him, as he helplessly tried to push and pinch his way out of it—the real Stephen was curled like a fetus inside the sheath of his body, waiting to be delivered.

"I don't know how to help you," his mother responded. "I suspect there's nothing to be done."

"But your own kid is being attacked!"

"You're better than they are, Stephen," she said firmly. "And that should be of some comfort to you."

"How would you like somebody making fun of something about *you*?" he said, under his breath.

"What do they make fun of?" she asked.

He remained silent for a moment, then spilled it. "My proboscis," he said.

She tilted her head back and looked at him steadily, the way she stared down at the toddlers while palpating their abdomens.

"Ignore them," she said finally.

They had a Dutch au pair when they first moved to Champaign, an unhappy ruddy-cheeked dental student who once fell down the stairs with the vacuum cleaner, arriving at the bottom with the wind knocked completely out of her. Stephen saw it all, the struggle to get the heavy machine down the stairs, the uncooperative hose smacking her in the face as she lugged the canister along, the simultaneous tangling of the cord and barking of the ankle, the missed tread, the cartwheeling of girl and machine, the two distinct thuds—her and then the vacuum on top of her.

Stephen was the smartest kid in his class, always, and the strangest.

For a long, imprinting moment, she stared at Stephen from the gleaming mahogany floor, crimson-faced except for the white rage spots forming under each eye, mouth opening and closing in the lull before her lungs filled with air. Years later, when he would see depictions in the movies of women in labor bearing down for the final push, he would flash back to the sprawled Dutch girl regaining her breath and bellowing at him in pain and frustration, yanking her hair and pounding her heels against the carpeted steps.

Since this ended up being his most vivid memory from childhood, it probably paved the way for his later entanglements with a series of short-fused foreign women. All doctoral students, all specializing in some sort of criticism, mostly of him. By the time he got to the last one, he had more or less worked through his fear of being yelled at in an accent. That one, Mette, didn't even come close to breaking his heart; in fact he was glad to be rid of her, a sharp-featured Norwegian beauty with food issues and a predilection for bickering, even about things he agreed with her on.

She was hollow-boned and elegant, very blonde (everywhere), with a delicate, feline face. She dressed carelessly, in clothing meant to be slid into and out of like a pair of clogs—soft shirts that gaped open alarmingly, revealing the bas-relief of her clavicle, knee-length skirts that swirled when she moved, and, sometimes, a pair of sagging argyle socks. For a while he couldn't stop looking at her, while she slept, read, rode in his truck, or reached behind her head and flipped her hair around in practiced moves that produced either two milkmaid-style braids or a smooth chignon. She cooked gourmet meals, swishing around his kitchen in her thick socks and thin skirt, the profile of one small red-tipped breast winking into view each time she moved.

"You are much less intelligent than most people believe," she would say, crushing walnut meats with the side of her knife and tossing them into a skillet.

> He liked to walk along, those evenings, thinking idly about science or sex.

She threw up dinner with a businesslike flexing of the chin and a few short ratchety coughs. Out it would come, in a long efficient strand, like a cat dislodging a hairball. She had no shame over it, either, but that didn't mean anything; she had once sat down to defecate while he was standing at the bathroom sink shaving.

After a decent interval, he broke up with her. She raised her eyes from the magazine she was reading and stared at him.

"You are brecking with me?" she asked. It was rhetorical, he knew better than to answer. "But Stephen. You are such a stinking piece of shit." She lifted her long arms over her head and gently twisted to the right, a yoga stretch, and then to the left. "A useless turd, and it's certain you will die alone, awake, and filthy in circumstances."

He still saw her at the co-op from time to time, carrying a thin bunch of organic carrots to the checkout, or trailing a pale hand along the granola bins. Once as he moved past her she whispered something so obscene and ungrammatical it stayed in his head for days.

It was right around then that he ended up with Aiko, who for all her difficulties had thrown up in front of him just one time, the front third of a bucktoothed underground creature that wasn't part of the catch and release program. And not that it was anyone's business, but he and the dog slept together easily, on their backs with a foot of gritty sheet between them.

In the early evening Stephen would trade one lab for the other; leaving his experiments percolating, he would race home to get Aiko out of the yard and then drive back up the hill, where they took long contemplative walks alongside the creeks and through the gorges of the Cornell campus.

Following her on the leash was no more possible than holding on to the bumper of a departing car; he went from that to a sixteen-foot rope wrapped around his right hand and pulled taut as a guy-wire. With Nathan's one-word texted blessing (whatever), he decided to let her run free. That first time, they sat in the cab of his truck for three minutes, Stephen laying down the law while Aiko stared straight ahead through the windshield.

"And I mean it, you *come* when you're called, Aiko. Aiko, *come*," he practiced. She refused to look in his direction even when he tugged her head around to face him.

He opened the driver's door and she was overtop of him and gone before he could do anything but clutch his gonads. While he sat in the truck, trying to think what to do, she came barreling back into view, stopped short, ears lifted up off her head, and crouched with her rump in the air. When he got out, she tore off again, returning as he rounded the first bend.

He liked to walk along, those evenings, thinking idly about science or sex, the joy of the bounding dog infecting his own life. It all seemed good, the experiments sputtering and dying in the petri dishes, the other experiments that yielded results his graduate students would carefully pen into a notebook, the muted pint-sized grandeur of the Ithaca landscape, with its plummeting overlooks, hanging bridges, and moody, hopeless skies.

It was a long way from California, the place he considered home, where they had moved him in the summer between fifth and sixth, and where he was miraculously reborn as just another kid with a banana seat bike. He went to a big California high school where everyone had a gimmick; his was that he was exceptionally smart. People called him Steve, without italics.

During college he discovered the Grateful Dead and that horizontal gene transfer occurred in plant cells from mitochondria to chloroplasts. One led to dope-driven guitar lessons and the other to much, much acclaim in the field of plant genetics. Eventually, he was able to combine the two, and wore tie-dye in his own lab.

Toward the end of their walk, while he was musing along, Aiko would occasionally bolt, right up the wall of the gorge, leaping from nothing to nothing, like a mountain goat, until she disappeared into the brush at the top. A moment later he'd see her dime-sized yellow face staring down at him before she took off for Frat Row, where groups of Greeks held barbecues on the lawns. She would trot into their midst and steal bratwursts off the fire or out of their hands, gulping them as she ran.

Stephen would have to drive from mansion to mansion on his way home, peering into the throngs of backward-capped boys and lean-hipped girls, all of them holding plastic cups of beer. If Aiko hung around and Stephen didn't show up, they would take out their phones and call him.

"Dude, your dog," they would say.

When Stephen was home from college one summer, eating breakfast in his parents' kitchen, there was a knock on the door. His father got up, went down the hall, and opened it. Without a word, he closed the door and walked back to the table, sat down and picked up his newspaper. There was a pause, and then another knock. Eleanor got up and went down the hall. She returned with a guy who looked exactly like Stephen's dad.

This was Morris's son from his first marriage, abandoned with the wife at the three-year mark, named Stephen. Eleanor was calm and relatively unsurprised; she'd been writing support checks to the ex-wife on this young man's behalf for more than twenty years. She sat him down with a stack of pancakes.

"Your name is *Stephen Klein?*" Stephen Klein asked him, appalled. This was the first he was hearing of any of it, and the guy had bristling eyebrows and exactly, *exactly* the same face as his dad.

"It is," the other Stephen said quietly. He looked at Eleanor with a kind of reverence, and picked up his fork, began eating.

"C?" Stephen's middle name was Charles.

"M." The first Stephen's middle name was Morris.

Morris, by this point, was gone, out of the room, out of the house, somewhere else. Stephen C. could never remember. What he did remember is that he spent the day with the older brother, getting high and showing him San Diego, and then at the end of the day the brother went home on a bus, back to some little town in Ottawa, and nobody ever mentioned him again.

Over the course of the summer, Stephen gave up on a lawn, and by fall on the concept of grass in general. By early winter the backyard was frozen into stark midwestern-looking furrows. Aiko enjoyed the cold as much as Stephen, and rode with him to the hockey rink every morning at 5:30. Once there, she fell back asleep across the seat while he tried to cover the net for an hour or so—the joyous wintertime sounds of ice being carved by skates, the scrape of the sticks, the muffled shouts. Afterward, the intramural handshakes, the steamed windows of the truck cab and the yellow dog's greeting, his goalie gear dumped in the mudroom, where it would gently exhale its stench all day.

It never stopped snowing, stinging evaporating needles of lake effect, and the white sky seemed to begin right above the roofline, creating the coldly claustrophobic pre-suicide atmosphere that Ithaca was known for. By mid-November the campus gorges were iced over like luge runs and the parks opened to the hunters—the paramilitary crossbow season was followed by the more standard Jack-in-the-thermos shotgun season, which was followed by the season of starved and staggering deer.

Once when he and Aiko were taking a turn around a pond in early winter she skidded out onto the ice and broke through, yelping and drowning. Heart thudding against his breastbone, Stephen had to stretch out like a starfish on the groaning surface and heave her up onto the ice. She rolled over, staggered to her feet, and then took off running, tail tucked. Hours after nightfall he was still searching, driving around with his frozen head out the window, shouting. Finally he saw her, curled up on a sprung sofa on the veranda of a frat house. She listened while he called her quite a few times, slapping the side of the truck for emphasis, before she stood up slowly, stretched fore and aft, and ambled out to see what he wanted.

The next day Nathan called. He was ready for his dog back.

Over the course of the summer, Stephen gave up on a lawn, and by fall on the concept of grass in general.

He missed her semi-desperately once she was gone, but the worst of it passed in a few days. It was like having a girlfriend leave, the agony of the clanging silence juxtaposed with the ecstasy of eating takeout burritos over the sink. With Aiko gone, weekends were the hardest, staying in bed too long, staring through the skylight at the milky clouds.

On Saturdays he always showered with his orchids, standing carefully amid the clay pots, steaming himself awake, and then rode his bicycle up the steep icy hill to campus. At the lab, thankfully, weekends were the same as weekdays—lank people in unfashionable clothes hunched over the bench, the morning smell of burned coffee gradually segueing into the afternoon smell of microwave popcorn. They all had interior lives, he could tell by the things they taped to their office doors, but it hardly ever leaked out in their dealings with him.

For a while he would just wander around, looking over their shoulders, asking questions, making his own set of notes. Then, when they were totally freaked out and nervous—he didn't mean for them to be, of course—he settled himself on a high stool to begin staring into a microscope, dividing cells with a delicate, threadlike tool. This was precision work not that many people knew how to do. He'd been trained by a French researcher, Yvonne, in a dark Paris laboratory. He had lived there for a year on a Guggenheim, rollerblading across town to the wrought-iron gates of the Scientific de Technologies; the elderly Yvonne waiting for him in her sensible shoes and low-cut smock. He placed one slide after another in the frame of the scope, and created a series of strands on each.

So actually he could probably scratch that idea, that people thought he was gay.

By the time he looked up, the place would be empty, the equipment robed, the fluorescents buzzing. Going home, his was always the only bike on the snowy hill, a long rocketing plummet in the dark. Once there, he got stoned and fooled around the house, stirring up the compost worms, tinkering with the downstairs toilet, hanging idly from the chin-up bar.

After the second weekend by himself, he decided to invite people over. There were two graduate students who could carry on conversations that weren't based on *Star Wars*, and there was Thor, his best friend from hockey, Thor's girlfriend, Chris, a lesbian-seeming redhead, there was Deirdre, a technical writer who lived down the street and watered his plants when he traveled, and the tuneless hummer, an Israeli visitor who was collaborating with him on a paper.

He would try to keep it from being one of his famous desultory dinner parties, forced marches through vegetarian terrain, with concert tapes of the Dead playing in the background. He would correct the most obvious errors from last time—he'd turn the heat up and put the worms in the basement. He'd get ketchup.

No one minded that he was preparing a seitan dish; the clouds had been hanging so low over Ithaca for so long that people were willing to entertain any notion. Everyone said yes and Deirdre wanted to bring a friend, which caused him a little twinge of regret, since he had considered going out with her if things didn't pick up. It seemed possible she thought he was gay because of the orchids, and he had imagined revealing otherwise, scattering a little surprise across her smooth white face. Although, it was true she had seen him with Mette, and, now that he thought about it, maybe with Sigrid, too. Sigrid had been hard to miss, a keyed-up flame-haired girl who wore an eye patch for a while due to a racquetball injury. So actually he could probably scratch that idea, that people thought he was gay.

Anyway, Deirdre left a message saying she would bring a friend unless he called and told her not to, and Thor left a message saying he wanted to bring another date besides Chris, but that Chris wanted to come too, they had stayed friends, etc. All this voicemail enthusiasm made Stephen feel as though he had already entertained, causing him to forget about the party completely until the very last minute, past the last minute, in fact.

He tried to do too many things in one day was the problem, and none of them pertaining to a dinner party. So he didn't make it to the co-op before it closed, he didn't refrigerate the cheesecake for the suggested six hours, and he didn't allot any time for showering. In the final moments before their arrival, the slab of seitan was thawing on a radiator, the dishwasher had chugged to a stop, and decorator cheeses were settling into a warm slump on a brightly colored Portuguese plate. There was a spectral dusting of flour in his hair and on his shirt, but a successful batch of homemade noodles hung everywhere in the kitchen, like soft damp worms.

Oops. He grabbed the compost box and ran it to the basement; while he was down there the front door banged open and what sounded like the entire party pushed its way into his foyer like a herd of steers, milling and stamping the snow off their feet. He crept up the basement stairs, listening to his guests greet one another, and then tiptoed back down again, peeling off his dirty shirt. He sorted quickly through the hockey-tainted pile of clothes at the mouth of the laundry chute—this morning's jersey had opened like a rank parachute over the entire stack—and then hurriedly put the original shirt back on. At the top of the stairs he realized it was backward, Bob Marley's face between his shoulder blades. As he pulled his arms out of the sleeves and shrugged it around, the basement door opened.

. . .

She had moved to Ithaca from Iowa City with her dog. They lived pictur-
esquely at the edge of a wood, in a shingled cottage surrounded by pine
trees and deer paths. It was like living in a snow globe, a silent scene that
you shake up only to watch the snow swirl and settle again, on the trees,
the roof, the rural mailbox. On the rare days that the sun shone, she would
emerge from the silent house and climb the hill to the shed, load wood
onto a child's sled, a yellow plastic saucer, and then give it a push. The sau-
cer would slide down the snow-packed slope, revolving, coming to rest
against the foundation of the house. She wore a wool hat that made her
forehead itch, and a long coat that was like an arctic sleeping bag with
sleeves. The small brown dog, picking her way along the top of drifts, cast
a lavender shadow. The dog was elderly and cheerful, the firewood was
heavy.

Night arrived in late afternoon, the woodburning stove creating a cir-
cle of oppressive heat in the living room, leaving the other rooms dark and
chilled, like the interior of a closed refrigerator. She didn't hate it, but she
didn't like it much either. There was nobody bothering her, true, but even-
tually, she was discovering, people need to be bothered. Her job wasn't
even full-time, didn't pay well, and was nearly as isolating as her house—
she worked alone in a tiny office at Cornell, managing a social psychology
journal whose editor was across campus in another department, where he
conducted his research and performed his teaching duties.

Nobody in her building knew her or what she was doing there, and the
only people who spoke to her were those who stood in the courtyard by
the mailroom a few times a day, to smoke cigarettes. Her own smoking had
increased to madwoman, to inpatient levels, ever since coming to Ithaca
in the late summer. Slowly, over many weeks, she formed a bond with
another smoker, a pretty young woman named Alana, with mall bangs and
fiercely pressed blue jeans, whose twin sister was dying of lymphoma in
Florida. She asked after the sister every few days and Alana would report
the latest, shaking her head in disbelief and resignation, sometimes crying,
sometimes turning her cigarette around to stare into its fiery end.

"It ain't good," she would say, stubbing her smoke against the side of
the building and running a finger under each eye. Alana worked in the
mailroom with two men, cutups, who worried about her behind her back
but were only able to joke. They were no help to Alana during the long
afternoons of sorting and thinking, her own face rising up in front of her,
jaundiced and suffering, her own head, grimly bald.

Nobody ever asked Joan anything about herself, because nobody cared. People back home somewhat cared, but not here in New York. Her own relatives didn't get her situation—they all understood her to be living in New York City. The ones who did seem to follow that she was in Ithaca thought it was a suburb of Manhattan.

"It's five hours from the city," she told her uncle at her goodbye party.

"Let me ask you," he said, narrowing his eyes. He considered himself worldlier than the others, a short-haul truck driver who frequently drove into the Loop in Chicago. "How far are you from Central Park?"

"Five hours," she said. "Five hours away. It's Ithaca, Uncle George, which is across the entire state from New York City."

"Do me a favor, listen to your old uncle," he told her. "Stay out of Central Park at night. There's nothing in there you need."

Nobody ever asked Joan anything about herself, because nobody cared.

Her park was called Treman, its upper entrance less than a mile from her house, and she and the dog hiked there every day, descending through damp granite that led to a series of narrow passages and jumbled steps past a foaming waterfall. From the shadows, the falls looked like an endless supply of milk being poured down a drain. At the bottom was a small footbridge with the word SMILE gouged into its railing, the S made with three straight lines, like a lightning bolt, or a Nazi symbol. She took these walks partly to get away from smiling, and would frown her way through the boggy acre of skunk cabbage, through the damp field of ferns where they had once seen a garter snake with its mouth unhinged, swallowing a frog, and then onto the steep switchback trail that led through the forest. Every day they did the four-mile loop, the dog double-time, running ahead and then back to check on her progress, both of them panting along. They rarely passed anyone, unless you counted the trees, tall and good-natured, their gnarled roots man-spread over the path.

She liked to think of nothing except what she was doing, following the plumy tail of the dog. This foot, that foot, this foot, that foot, this foot, that foot, this foot, that foot, this one, that one, this one, that one, this one, that one, this one, that one, this, that, this, that, this, that, this, that, this, that, until eventually there was nothing but the path, and the occasional thought scudding across the blue sky of her mind. It was everything she had wanted when she came to Ithaca, and less.

She had enjoyed her life back in Iowa City up to a point, working for a space physics journal at the university, living with her husband and their dogs in an old house surrounded by oak trees. She liked the scientists, their amiability and their focus, the way they understood complicated, invisible things but didn't understand simple ones, like regular hair washing or why a paper called "The Effect of the Giant Thruster on the Spread-F Region" was funny.

> She had liked her friends in Iowa, not up to a point but forever.

She had liked her marriage too, up to a point, that being when her husband left her for one of their friends. She had a minor nervous breakdown from the surprise of it and from the yawning chasm that opened up inside her. One morning she called her sister from the bathtub, weeping into a washcloth, unable to speak. Her sister drove over from the town where they had grown up, sixty miles away, and sat on the closed toilet lid with her legs crossed, sorting through a shoe box of pharmaceuticals she'd brought with her, looking for divorce pills. By this time, Joan was out of the tub, sitting on the edge, wrapped in a towel.

"Here we go," her sister said. "These make you feel like melting butter."

She gave one pill to herself and one to Joan, and they ended up sleeping the whole afternoon, sprawled in the same bed, like when they were kids.

She had liked her friends in Iowa, not up to a point but forever, the women who supported her through her divorce, the same women she had supported through theirs. They ranged anywhere from bossy ("Think about yourself, not about him") to unrealistic ("You will never regret this but he will") to hopeful ("This is your get out of jail free card") to mystical ("The hanged man actually is a positive card") to useful ("Where do you keep your booze?"). They helped her move all the stuff he left behind to the garage and then made a bonfire in the backyard of the farmhouse and milled around declaring it her year while she shivered in a lawn chair with her knees drawn up, wearing a cruddy down vest liberated from one of the boxes.

And then someone else took over the space journal and she found herself working for a professor emeritus who spent his days in an office on the top floor of a building named after him, pottering around and giving orders to his half-retired secretary, an elderly woman named Mrs. P who wore dark glasses for an eye condition and loud perfume. Every morning there were more emails from scientists, asking the status of their papers, queries that the professor emeritus took long hours to ponder and then answered in circuitous letters filled with courtliness and spin, which Mrs. P laboriously typed and mailed out, using her own roll of stamps instead of the franking machine.

Joan got sick of it eventually, the divorce pain, the chasm, the switching from the old editor, who did things like ask her what she was reading, and the new editor, who did things like ask her to bring him coffee. The first time, she had said yes because she was taken by surprise, the second time because she wanted a cup for herself, the third time because she felt solidarity with Mrs. P, who would have to go up and down the stairs in her place, and the fourth, fifth, and sixth times because his name was in the dictionary.

One of the guys had rigged it so that when she turned on her printer each morning it would chug out a piece of paper with a daily quote on it. Once it said, "Politicians make strange bedfellows," and she had folded it, put it in a university envelope, and mailed it to her ex-husband, who was a local politician. She used the franking machine. Another time it said, "Sometimes you find yourself in the middle of nowhere, and sometimes in the middle of nowhere you find yourself," attributed to Jerry Garcia, her old favorite. One morning, it said, "Traveler, there is no path; paths are made by walking," and instead of recycling it, she put it on her desk and looked at it. *Traveler, there is no path; paths are made by walking.* Anonymous had said it, and she was right.

The Russians arrived on time, stubbled and hungover, two of them in the cab of a cross-country moving truck. They were sipping from large cups of coffee and greeted her elaborately and—she thought—ironically. The packing materials that were supposed to be in the back of the already half-filled truck weren't there at all but sitting on the corrugated floor were two more guys, smoking and eating crusts out of a battered pizza box. The crew convened in a corner of her living room for twenty minutes, drinking their coffee and discussing in Russian how to pack a whole house with nothing but a phone book and her own laundry baskets. When she approached, one said, "Lady, this isn't for you to worry . . . we will have for you to worry later."

The Iowa City house was ornate and crumbly with high ceilings, pocket doors, and a resounding, barren echo. Most everything of value had been given to the ex, and nearly everything else had been dragged to the curb for university students to pick through. They rode up on bikes and steered carefully away, balancing crockery, birdcages, vintage vinyl (James Gang, Grateful Dead), garden rakes, faded quilts, antique egg crates. The rest of it went to the dump. She and her friend Sara, stoned and eating potato chips, drove a borrowed pickup truck to the landfill, where they hurled her belongings onto the spongy ground, Sara bursting into tears finally, saying, "Even this? Even these?" as she threw objects and boxes of objects over the side. When they pulled away, an idling bulldozer came forward and pushed a wave of dirt over the whole mess as Sara leaned out the window, spellbound and dismayed.

So, Joan had erased her past, but still the paltry present had to be packed, so she drove to the grocery store and filled her hatchback with a stack of soiled produce boxes and some flattened cartons held together with twine. Back at the house, the head mover produced a large roll of tape from the cab of the truck and held it triumphantly above his head.

A shirtless blond guy in dress pants was packing the entire contents of her kitchen using the yellow pages. He placed one page between each of her plates, like a bookmark. "Why are you even bothering?" she asked him.

"Lady, we must *pack*," he said, gesturing dynamically and rolling his eyes. "Lady think she can move without pack." In her bedroom, one guy was halfheartedly dumping shoes and books into the same flimsy box, while another stared pensively into the drawer from her bedside table.

As soon as they had jammed her stuff onto the truck, the movers drove off to their next destination, wherever that was, all four of them in the cab. She handed her house key to the real estate agent and said goodbye to her friends, who stood in the street and waved after her, a row of women with bright frightened smiles on their faces, just like the one on hers.

It was August and hot, and she left on Highway 6, a narrow two-lane that ran through the treeless, endless landscape of corn. The sun and wind blasted into the driver's side window, and fifteen minutes out there was an accident on the road. Her car was the third in line, stopped by a motorist waving a white dress shirt. Just beyond him was the wreck itself, a sports car resting upside down in a ditch, and an SUV, lodged against a crumpled guardrail, its unbent grill glinting fearlessly. She couldn't look at the accident, so she and the dog got out and stared behind them, watching the line of cars increasing one by one, clicking into place like a row of dominos.

Eventually, a chopper appeared, dangling from its propeller, and settled awkwardly on the pavement up ahead. It took on cargo and then spun up and away, veering over the line of cars, hovered uncertainly for a moment, and then swept westward. Traffic resumed, chastened, crawling across the landscape in a long slow line, like a caterpillar consuming a leaf.

In the late summer and early fall, Ithaca truly did live up to its bumper stickers—it was gorges. The park's narrow passageway opened onto her chasm, externalized so she could walk through it and come out the other side every afternoon. Her rustic house with its set of big glass doors looking out on the trees, the little dog sleeping in the crook of her arm at night, the part-time nature of her job allowing her to get up every morning and drink coffee while making drawings of her dreams, the good parking space at work, the bad people down the road who bred Dobermans and had mysterious gatherings that included scores of cars parked willy-nilly along the gravel. She decided to like the bad people

A shirtless blond guy in dress pants was packing the entire contents of her kitchen using the yellow pages.

because they pointed their guns at the ground when she drove by and also because she was afraid of them.

The premium parking space at Cornell was secured for her by the new boss, Ed, a man so kind and thoughtful that she suspected he might be paying some kind of monthly freight on it. Those were the two perks to her job—the parking space and Ed. Otherwise, it was deadly, sonorously dull, forcing people to crawl out of sleep in the morning and draw their dreams.

The social psychologists all seemed like perfectly regular, nice people, far enough away from the spectrum that they could study it. Writing long laborious papers proving that people who lived alone and had fewer social contacts were lonelier than those who lived with others and had a social life. Conducting extensive NSF-funded experiments instead of just calling her.

Her Iowa friends didn't abandon her. A couple of them checked in every day or so, just to talk about nothing.

"How's the Pink Eddie factory?" Mary would ask. Ed occasionally wore a pink polo shirt with his khakis. "What's new in squishiology?"

It was a soft science, true, but civilized in a way that astrophysics hadn't been. Nobody ever fainted, for instance, from staring too long into a telescope. Nobody ever brought her inappropriate gifts or accidentally wore their wife's blouse to work. Nobody, in fact, ever did anything, including her.

"What's your plan for the weekend?" Pat would ask each Friday.

Her weekend plan was mostly: on Saturday draw, hike, go to the co-op, get Thai takeout, watch a movie, read; on Sunday draw, hike, go to the mall, get Thai takeout, watch a movie, read. The mall was in Syracuse, the nearest city with sunlight, and she would drive the interstate for an hour-plus until she saw its carousel roof, and then wander around Lord & Taylor in her hiking boots, looking at clothes until she felt like herself again. Then she would drive back.

Once Pat had to remind her that they were coming up on a three-day weekend and she broke down in tears, right at her desk. It turned out okay, because she cleaned her fridge on the third day and then drove twenty miles to Taughannock Park, which had its own falls, a tall narrow ribbon of silver that emptied into a deep pool at the bottom. She found a ledge and read her book, checking the time every ten minutes or so, while Sheba walked around on the mossy rocks. After one hour they got Thai takeout and went home.

> Before she could formulate a plan her father came down with a terrible flu that turned out to be cancer.

It started snowing and wouldn't stop. It didn't always accumulate, but it always snowed, sometimes invisibly, just the feeling of straight pins being hurled at her face. Men in camouflage began materializing in the park—one time she saw a thermos hovering in the air, silver with a blue plastic cap, before realizing it was strapped to a hunter, holding a crossbow and leaning against a tree, observing her.

"I wouldn't let your dog get too far ahead," he said as she passed.

One of the dreams she had drawn was of being pierced through by an arrow. In the dream, it hadn't hurt, but she couldn't pull it out because it was barbed, like a cupid's arrow. In the drawing, she was sort of hunched over it, wearing a nightgown, and had a black bar over her eyes, the way they did in old girlie magazines. She had thought the dream might be trying to tell her something, which it was. Like, stop going to the park.

She threw herself into piecework at the Pink Eddie factory, sending the papers out to reviewers at a blinding clip, retrieving their responses and walking briskly across campus to share them with Ed, even going to dinner at his house with his wife, who was warm and lovely, and a postdoc from Korea and his wife, who also was warm and lovely, although she barely spoke English and once when she thought no one was looking glared at the coffee table and ran her hand through her hair in a mad housewife way.

Right around then the snow started accumulating, banks of it, stiff like packing material that creaked when she walked on it. The gray smoke from her chimney dispersed into the gray sky and she countered by buying an elaborate set of bright markers. They stood upright in their own plastic lazy Susan, taking up half her drawing table, every possible hue of every primary color. One time somebody sent her a boxed set of *Beavis and Butt-Head* DVDs and she watched all of them in a row on a dim Saturday, and then threw up her pad thai. Another time she tried to walk her dog on the road and was accosted by the Dobermans. Sheba, mostly blind, was still willing to kill them, spinning in circles and making exorcist noises. The Dobermans followed, their hackles raised, growling.

"Can you please call your fucking *dogs off*?" she cried to the people, who were standing in their yard watching.

"Muffin," the woman said, after a moment. "Trina."

The dogs took a few more stiff-legged steps and then turned and trotted back to their house and up the driveway.

It was around this time that she began to think about making some friends.

Before she could formulate a plan her father came down with a terrible flu that turned out to be cancer. For a few weeks, her sister ferried him to radiation and chemo, calling to report the details—the Sharpie diagrams drawn on his skin, the gruesome melted-chalk taste of the Ensure he drank from a bent straw, the waiting rooms with TVs blasting, Ellen dancing ghoulishly across the screen while patients shivered under afghans, receiving their poison.

Joan called him every day after his treatments, making her voice buoyant, and then again in the evening to see what he was having for dinner, even though he always said the same thing: "One of these milkshakes." Near the end of every conversation, as before, he would ask, "How's your little dog?" He never called her Sheba, even to her face.

The day he didn't answer she got hold of her sister, who drove over to find him collapsed on the floor.

"It's not going to work out," her sister whispered into the phone that evening, from the hospital corridor.

Within two hours, Joan and the dog were in the car, creeping on snowpack through western New York and then driving fast on dry pavement all through the night. Loud music and sparkling stars, until it was dawn in the Midwest, and they could slow down.

They had him sitting in a chair, but he was slumped over, eyes closed. He looked smaller, burnished, and so intensely like himself that for a moment, standing in the hall, Joan didn't recognize him. Next to him was Connie, one of his girlfriends, wearing a sweatshirt with a big plaid heart appliquéd on the front. Connie was looking at her shoes, turning them thoughtfully this way and that. She reached down into her bag of knitting, took out a long blue needle, and poked at the sole of one sneaker, dislodging something that she then picked up with a Kleenex and deposited in the wastebasket. While up, she tidied a stack of newspapers and then opened the drawer of the nightstand.

"Boy, they give you everything you need," she said.

He roused himself to agree with her, and shut his eyes again.

"Looky who's here!" Connie cried.

Joan started to feel a little unhinged when she knelt to hug him; he was ectoplasm. He raised one hand slowly, ran it ruminatively over his face, and then set it gently in his lap again. His legs looked severely compromised without trousers, wavery and slightly see-through. A phone rang loudly and everyone flinched.

"It's turned way up," Connie said. Her ride was calling from the lobby.

They walked to the elevator while a stout, uncheerful nurse tended to her father. Joan and her sister liked Connie the best out of all their dad's girlfriends, because she was the most like their long-dead mother—she liked to party but kept her wits about her. She was going to bingo that night, but would come back and sit with him the next afternoon. The elevator doors opened and Connie gave her a quick, hard hug before stepping in. They were both crying.

The nurse had helped him back into bed; the covers pulled formally up to his shoulders and then folded back. He was staring out the window to his left. From a standing position, the window looked out over a field of Mercedes Benzes and BMWs, the doctors' parking lot, but from the perspective of the prone patient, it was just blue sky and gorgeous pillowy midwestern clouds.

"Look at that sky, Dad," Joan said. He continued to gaze, his jaw moving imperceptibly, as though he were chewing something very small. She pulled up a chair and watched with him. The blue, the clouds, the occasional gliding bird. At some point she took his hand. He nodded, as though she'd said something, and continued gazing.

Her best friend from childhood drove over from Chicago for the funeral. They spent the night before making popcorn and drinking from the parents' liquor cabinet, just like high school, and then later slept in the twin beds in Joan's old bedroom, whispering in the dark the way they always had, even though there was no one to hear them.

Before they turned sixteen, they had made their dads drive them everywhere at all hours and their dads had done it without complaining, even though Liz's had only one arm, and Joan's was occasionally inebriated.

> Joan started to feel a little unhinged when she knelt to hug him; he was ectoplasm.

"They were the last decent guys," Liz whispered.

Joan and her sister had spent one afternoon, while Connie sat with their father, intending to go through the house and figure out what to do with things. Joan had opened the drawer of the buffet in the dining room where they kept the communal combs and brushes, bobby pins and barrettes, and in the very back found a brush with their mother's hair preserved in it, from long ago. Before death, before chemo even. The hairbrush defeated them entirely and they had found someone who would come dismantle the house and sell what could be sold.

After the service, after everything, Joan gathered two boxes of stuff from the attic and Sheba, then called her sister from the phone in the kitchen, lighting a cigarette and staring out the window, the way their mother used to do.

"That was fun experiencing another death with you," her sister said. "Let's do it again soon."

"Next time it can be mine," Joan said. "Just kidding."

"You need to make friends out there," her sister said. "Liz agrees. We discussed you."

"You don't disgust me," Joan said. Outside, a black squirrel was sniffing around under the tree.

"I mean it," her sister said. They were both their mother now.

The black squirrel came to the sliding glass door and put his front paws up on it, peering in. After they said goodbye, Joan filled all the feeders for the last time, found a jar of peanuts in the cupboard, and emptied it around the base of the tree.

"I filled your feeders, Dad," she called into the empty house, and then got in her car and drove back to Ithaca.

You are the universe in ecstatic motion. One of the Rumi signs wobbling on its nail.

She quit smoking once she got back, except for a couple of times a day, when she went down to stand in the alcove with Alana, whose sister had died during the three weeks Joan had been back home. They shivered companionably, backs against the cold stone of the building, not saying much, just watching the smoke as it hurried away from them, like everything else.

She started going to a yoga class where everyone was more flexible than her, and to a meditation class run by a super-crabby monk in a messy living room.

"I have to move shit off the rug to put my cushion down," she told Pat.

"Can't anyone say they're a monk?" Pat asked.

"I think they're real. They all live in that house and wear gowns," Joan told her.

Everyone in the meditation group seemed a bit off in some way, including her, but she liked closing her eyes and imagining the path through her park for forty-five minutes every Wednesday night. This foot, that foot, this foot, that foot. She liked the Rumi quotes in dime-store frames, hanging precariously on nails here and there. *Love is the bridge between you and everything.* This, that, this, that, until eventually there was nothing but the gray sky of her mind and the faint odor of the carpet.

Someone who worked in her building showed up at yoga class, a pale woman with bobbed hair, like a flapper's, and dark lipstick. It was her clothes that Joan had noticed more than the woman, as she went up the stairs past the journal office in the mornings. Billowy slacks and tailored dresses and narrow skirts with crisp blouses and once in the fall a soft belted jacket with felt flowers appliquéd on it that sounds terrible but wasn't. The last thing Joan would see, after the outfit went past, were the shoes—flats, ankle boots, and sometimes a pair of slender wingtips that looked like men's shoes except for the heels. The woman was quietly hopeless in yoga class; when they bent over to touch the floor, she was still basically upright.

"I refuse to do the sun salutation until there's a sun," Joan whispered to her as they were standing around, watching the others do headstands.

"I just had to get the fuck out of my house," the woman whispered back.

"Could we maybe do a tripod?" the teacher asked them gently. She was in her early seventies, and wore harem pants and a lavender leotard. She moved her topknot out of the way, put the crown of her head on the floor, balanced knees on elbows, and smiled at them upside down.

You are the universe in ecstatic motion. One of the Rumi signs wobbling on its nail.

Once in the tripod, Joan raised her legs slowly and balanced there, while the teacher stood behind her, just barely touching her ankles.

"I met someone," she told Mary the next day. "A woman in my building. Her name is Deirdre, she's a technical writer and when I asked what that meant, she goes, 'Well . . . it's technical,' i.e., sense of humor."

"I thought you were going to say a guy," Mary said. "But this is very good."

That afternoon on her way out, Deirdre stopped in Joan's office and invited her to go to a party over the weekend. Her neighbor was having it and Deirdre wouldn't really know anyone there except him.

"Who is he?" Joan asked.

"I'm not sure, just this guy scientist," Deirdre said. "He's kind of," and she made a waving gesture around her head. "He has a lot of plants in his house is all I know, and he rides a bike in the snow."

Joan was too shy to go to a party where she knew only one person slightly, because what if nobody talked to her. Then she remembered she was in Ithaca, where nothing mattered.

"Okay," she said.

On Saturday she loaded wood with Sheba and then they watched a movie in the afternoon, curled up together on the sofa while it snowed. When they woke, the sky had gone from tarnished spoon to black and Joan didn't have time to make herself look any better than usual.

It took forever to get the snow off her car, and she ended up leaving it with a tall crown on top that looked like a haircut from the eighties. She slid sideways down the big hill and then fishtailed into town, arriving at the address exactly when everyone else did. Somebody immediately parked behind her.

The house had a wide porch and carved front doors with bubbled glass, like an old Iowa farmhouse. The walk had been shoveled haphazardly and they picked their way up the steps and onto the porch and then a tall guy in a thick sweater banged on one of the doors, pushed it open, and they all herded inside.

There was an awkward stamping of snow off boots and smiling; everyone had hat-hair and was trying to do something about it.

"I'm Deirdre," Deirdre said.

A portly guy with a bushy beard said, "Ari."

"Chris," said a woman with short red hair, unzipping her coat. "This is Diane."

Diane said hello and then the tall, sweatered guy said, "Thor here."

"Joan."

The foyer was clean and empty, with apricot walls and a neat rag rug. Just beyond was a kitchen where she could see big bulbs of garlic hanging in a bunch over a butcher block, bright crockery on the open shelves, and a ladder-back chair with what looked like her mother's homemade noodles draped over its rungs. In a room off to the right were pots of ferns and orchids, a ficus tree with lights sparkling in the leaves, a scarlet begonia blooming next to a guitar in its stand, and a big gray sofa. There was music in the background that she recognized. Her old friend, Jerry Garcia.

Diane asked what they should do with their coats.

Ari pointed toward a closed door.

Once in a while you get shown the light. Joan felt the warmth of the house and the people radiating through her like home. It was the universe in ecstatic motion. There were two doors, actually, and she stepped forward and opened the right wrong one. ⬧

OF MY FURY

I love a man I know could die
And not by way of illness
And not by his own hand
But because of the color of that hand and all
His flawless skin. One joy in it is
Understanding he can hurt me
But won't. I thought by now I'd be unhappy
Unconscious next to the same lover
So many nights in a row. He readies
For bed right on the other side
Of my fury, but first, I make a braid of us.
I don't sleep until I get what I want.

VISTA

Couples new enough to believe
A house will make them happy
Go looking on long drives. It's Sunday.
These streets don't want
Black people. Folk need
Another bedroom because of another
Baby, or they need a koi pond
For no reason at all. And
Aren't our needs far from those
Who remind us what we look like?
I can't teach you how to love, but
I can show you who. I walk right
Past your yellow property, day-
Dreaming. Your yard is big enough.
Whatever I say gets said from the road.

FIRST CLASS

All the terrorists sit in first class
With the men who won't look at me
And the men who shouldn't,
With the men who say cat and mean
Vagina. That frivolity changes. Suddenly,
We're in the midst of an assassination,
And ain't that the bottom of a big bowl
Of disaster! Sick in it. Done of it. Why do we visit
Any grave? It's always too late. All that talk
About tomorrow, all that talk about Chicago,
The time spent testing fruit, which really meant
Finding sugar in disguise, the years I didn't know
What to do with my body, my head cradled
In the chiropractor's hands, how I paid my debts
Sleeping on an air mattress, how I straightened
My teeth and fixed my diction, my self-
Imposed halo, my vegan pride; when instead,
I should have snorted a line. I should have
Told the bitches I hate most what I practiced
In the mirror, *Sweetheart, I am not afraid*
Of you nor do I fear your ripe honey-mongering ways.
I should have asked the man I took this flight
To avoid, *What happens if I kiss you?* But here I am
Headed to earth among the screamers
Thinking of my little gray car parked and locked
In the airport lot. Who could drive it as I have?

GOOD MOTHER

Praise the woman who took me in her arms &
wouldn't let go of me. We sank to the floor
in the middle of the aisle in Rite Aid.
It was a late morning & I walked slowly,
furious that spring could still be so wonderful.
Magnolia tempted me to forget about my mother
for a few minutes. I stared at a Brooklyn blue sky
through the branches clasping pear blossoms.
The limbs shook in sunlight. My eyes adjusted
when I went into the pharmacy & realized
everywhere I looked the world announced
it would soon be Mother's Day. Something
ripped itself out of me. A howl so wide
I thought I would burst. The woman in the center
understood right away, the way my mother once understood
I had been born in a specific sadness.
She did not say she was a mother but I knew it.
She put her arms around me & waved away the cashiers,
the security guard who repeated *Ma'am? Ma'am?*
A stranger rocked me in her arms, so much kindness
as we fell over & crashed against a row of votive candles.
She didn't say it would be okay. She didn't ask me
what was wrong. But her arms put me in a vicious prayer.

I almost bit her, almost pushed her away.
We held on. We held on & praised the nameless thing
that makes us what we think we aren't strong enough
to know. She knew. She didn't let go of me.
Praise the woman who didn't wipe my snot from her shirt,
my tears from her collarbone, who did not tell me to
pull myself together while everything inside me dropped.
Crushed bones. Blossoms pushing through my mouth—
a word, *Mom Mom Mom*. This broken birdsong of mine
with no bird, no wing, no way to fly back through time.
Praise the woman who did not leave me
like something suddenly dead on the sidewalk
with a breeze blowing over its face.
Praise the woman who smelled like fabric softener
& coffee & the good things I must believe I am too.
Praise the mothers who walk slowly through the world,
bringing children into themselves, sometimes burying children
before themselves, & who defend something harder
than innocence. Praise the guts & grace of mothers.
Praise their exhaustion & their good work. Praise their wit,
their wonderful ways of listening to the world fall
asleep against its clean pillow. For the woman
who knelt with me in an ugly heap in the middle of

Rite Aid on an unbearable spring day,
who helped me buy a Mother's Day card
for my dead mother, who knew better than to say
I'd be just fine, for you I lift my arms each spring
& wish you a kindness so fantastic I sometimes feel
I'm in midair, the shadow of my wings clapping in joy
above your children, who must love you.

SEEING THE BODY: VOLUME

Fluid was the enemy of our house.
Always on guard my mother studied her
ankles & hands all the time. Any swelling
set off alarms. Everything in our house
bolted to wet silence. Our family
could be capsized should the fluid
breach her heart. More than once
it did. Surrounded her heart
with gold liquid. Attacked her
heart with its rising flood.
I hated the smell & arrogance
of it. The way it misshaped
my mother's lovely muscles.
I never understood how
the body made so much of it.
She would pull fluid off her body.
Worried for the kidney
she had received from a murdered child.
Worried that the fluid would pull her
under the hull of her own organs.
Liters & milliliters placed us
on the brink. For years after she died
I lived along a gold, slow edge

of *Maybe* or *Maybe Not*. I kept asking:
Could I have ever saved her sinking vessel?
I only mean that some days I was certain
there was nothing left after she died
that could fill the hollows in me. I wanted to know
how I could drown my Ishmael
of memory. Pull my life out of my mother's
mute grave. Nothing to surround my heart,
which turned & kicked like something
orphaned in its cradle. I got so sick in January
my doctors ordered multiple blood transfusions.
My blood was going bad, giving up its own air.
Yet I refused. I had given so much of
my blood to my mother's absence
I could barely stand to give myself
the anchor of blood that might pull me
above the waves, above those lost years I drifted
like an empty bottle upon the tide.

HER TATTOO IS MY NAME & MY NAME IS A POEM

Amy Lam

永世成佳岑

I traded a McDonald's two-cheeseburger extra-value meal for a tattoo over a decade ago. A friend permanently inked my parents' house key against my spine, in between my soft shoulder blades, as I hunched over a folding chair in a dining room with bad lighting. Afterward, in my old Corolla, I took us to the drive-through on a rare drizzly Los Angeles winter afternoon.

A couple of years before that, I made my then-boyfriend swear he wouldn't tell anyone I paid the tattoo shop's minimum of $50 for a simple drawing that didn't take longer than five minutes to sink into my skin. I was more embarrassed about having paid so much for the tattoo than about the tattoo itself. Fifteen years later, it's now a faded, blurry, red line sketch of a two-inch-tall pitchfork. A tiny triangle makes the small point at the end of each of the three prongs. The pitchfork points upward, standing just a few inches above my butt crack.

The pitchfork and the house key are two of the seven tattoos on my body. Each of their creations was a vibrating catharsis, proof of a feeling—a time stamp rather than a tramp stamp. Some of them are reminders to myself—saturated with

history and aspirations. Some of them are more like a pitchfork above my ass.

So I'm familiar with the impulsive desire to offer a part of yourself to a stranger with electric needles and a rainbow of inks. I understand that desire to stake claim to your own flesh. Many of us have made rash, regrettable decisions marked by permanence—it's just some of us did it with tattoos. And yet, I still don't understand why people get Chinese characters tattooed on them when they don't know the difference between 媽 and 馬.

• • •

In April 2016, Holland Christensen told strangers on the internet about her Chinese tattoo. That wasn't her intention when she posted anonymously to a popular basketball forum. The /r/NBA subreddit is a place known for discussing player stats and sharing highlight clips, with approximately 360,000 subscribers at the time—myself among them. It isn't the place to look for a game-day buddy. Still, Christensen submitted a post entitled "Hornets Fans help! I have no one to go with me to the game vs. the Nets tonight, extra ticket is free!"

"The tickets are good seats, and I would give you my extra one for free in exchange for your company," she wrote. "I'm pretty awesome to be around."

Christensen was desperate. At the last minute, a friend had canceled plans to attend the game with her, but Christensen needed to see the Charlotte Hornets play. She had recently decided that she would become the biggest fan of the team's second-string point guard, Jeremy Lin—after unknowingly having his Chinese name tattooed on her.

Christensen, who is originally from the small town of Jasper, Tennessee, had not known who Jeremy Lin was until after his name became a part of her. She discovered that the three boxy Chinese characters stacked in a neat column on her left ankle wrote his name, 林書豪. A few days following the /r/NBA post, she uploaded a twelve-minute video to YouTube, simply titled "Accidental Jeremy Lin Tattoo."

In the video, Christensen sits in front of a colorful, abstract cityscape poster pinned to a pink wall, her straight blond hair under a gray knit cap. Her southern accent pulls long vowels and *Lin* is rendered a two-syllable word. She admits it was a "complete basic white girl tattoo."

• • •

Jeremy Lin's second NBA season, in 2011–12, could have been his final season in the league. Though he made headlines as a Cinderella story in 2010, when, as an undrafted rookie, he eventually earned a spot with his hometown Golden State Warriors, the Harvard grad was hardly on anyone's radar as a breakout player. After a stint in the D-League, a few games in the Chinese Basketball Association in the off-season, and a couple of preseason showings with the Houston Rockets before being waived by the team, he landed with the New York Knicks at the very end of 2011. Lin has since shared in interviews that he was sleeping on his brother's couch in NYC, the unglamorous reality of an athlete trying to create a sustainable *pro*-athlete life. He has told the story of heading into Madison Square Garden for practice, like the rest of his team, and being stopped and questioned by security, who couldn't fathom he was a point guard—an actual basketball player.

> I'm familiar with the impulsive desire to offer a part of yourself to a stranger with electric needles and a rainbow of inks.

PHOTO: ON HEAVENLY MOUNTAIN (TIANZI SHANSHANG) 1998 (WOODCUT), WU JUNFA (B.1927) / PRIVATE COLLECTION / BRIDGEMAN IMAGES

But in February 2012—like the third act of a feel-good film about hard work, redemption, and never giving up on yourself—Lin made an upswing and spurred a phenomenon dubbed Linsanity. He became the hero in an (Ivy league) rags-to-riches story of how he led the New York Knicks on a seven-game winning streak following a dismal record of losing at 8–15. Lin, who grew up playing basketball in California, was a version of the middle-school boys I watched dribble up and down cracked blacktop playgrounds on the hot Los Angeles afternoons of my own childhood. He took up space in an arena where Asian Americans had not seen our bodies celebrated in this way—the exception being Yao Ming, who played for the Houston Rockets for almost a decade, ending in 2011. Yao was singular at seven and a half feet tall, a Chinese national who barely spoke English when he was the number-one draft pick in 2002, whereas Lin is an approximation of us, similarly rooted in the nebulous state of Asian America, a place where diasporic Asians are fluent in America but that fluency isn't returned, where we aren't granted full admission into the spaces we call home.

As Linsanity grew that spring, I could feel my own stupor lift. I had been wrestling with a mental health crisis, a depression that had me imagining comfort in the cool soil in an overgrown vacant field. Watching an entire city celebrate Lin offered a semblance of buoyancy to my days. I scrolled through eBay contemplating whether I should spend my unemployment money on his sold-out #17 jersey, even though my wardrobe had never been home to a sports jersey. I was compelled to consider it not so much because this felt like a significant cultural moment for Asian Americans, but more because this was the first time I had seen an approximation of my name emblazoned on people's backs and I wanted to remember it this way.

Imagine conflating ignorance with exoticism, thinking yourself deep for branding your flesh with a language you don't know.

. . .

Lin is the child of Taiwanese immigrants, while I am the child of Vietnamese refugees. Lin's parents arrived in America to attend university, while my family arrived here as a consequence of war. Lin earned a degree in economics from Harvard, while I once bought a crimson red sweater with HARVARD across the chest for $1.99 from a thrift store. Our commonality begins and ends here: we're both of the Chinese diaspora and our family name is 林. The thing about being part of a diaspora is that you grasp at anything that will help you feel as if you belong to a tribe. And now I'm in a tribe where my family name is tattooed on a white lady's ankle, like a souvenir to a place she has never been.

. . .

Chinese and Japanese character tattoos have recently gone out of fashion, which is an odd thing to say since the wearers of them can't take them off. Kanji tattoos reached peak popularity in the 1990s–2000s. Hanzi Smatter was a popular blog of the time, perfect for a tattoo rubbernecker like myself. Here, the tattooed, or friends of the tattooed, emailed a Chinese-born college student in the US to confirm or disprove the meaning of a tattoo. Of course the blog was a photo album of botched kanji, pure gibberish characters, and terribly translated phrases.

I asked the artist who gave me my most recent tattoo about the bygone trend. I saw Amanda Meyers in the spring of 2008, when she put a bookmark on my chest. She began tattooing in 1991 and still owns a shop in Portland, Oregon, though she stopped tattooing in 2013. I recalled how many American tattoo shops in the 2000s had sheets of flash art made up of kanji and clichéd designs of thorny roses and Celtic armbands to choose from. Meyers said customers were less likely to ask for a custom piece: "A lot of people didn't know to think of their own thing." She believes most customers who chose kanji tattoos imbued them with spirituality and exoticism—and who was she to say no? She had bills to pay.

Imagine conflating ignorance with exoticism, thinking yourself deep for branding your flesh with a language you don't know. Was I unfamiliar with this desperation of seeking home in words I could not read or write? I am of the diaspora, after all.

A 2010 masters dissertation by a University of Toronto student, Karen Bic Kwun Chan, asks questions about the legibility of Chinese-character tattoos and their relationship to Chinese people living in diaspora. In "Chinese Enough For Ya?: Disrupting and Transforming Notions of Chineseness through Chinesenough Tattoos," Chan purposefully renames kanji tattoos. She coins the term "Chinesenough," which she explains like this:

> Not quite "Chinese" but passing for Chinese in the mainstream, "Chinesenough" corresponds to simulacra that bear enough markers to be recognized as Chinese by dominant society, and enough markers to be recognized as distinctly not-Chinese, literally, by some others.
>
> Chinesenough as a notion, however, is itself a paradox. Chinesenough things are *both* Chinese and not-Chinese, and at the same time, they are *neither*.

Chan's dissertation names the sliver of a liminal space between meaning and nothingness—not just in a bad tattoo. The concept of Chinesenough feels like a biography for so many of us who "bear enough markers to be recognized" as Asian, seldom as American, and rarely feel like *enough* of either.

. . .

My father named me 林正麗.

林, or Lin, or Lam. Our family name means *forest* because our ancestors came from the woods of southern China; 林 is made of two pieces of wood, or 木. My given name, the one my parents and elders call me, is 麗. On Saturday mornings, my parents sent me to Chinese school in a small Buddhist temple in Los Angeles's Chinatown. I was four years old and learned to write my given name in its simplified form, 丽. When I was about ten years old, I asked my father what my given name means and he pointed to the traditional character in a Chinese-English dictionary. My name means *beautiful*—I was unsure if this was the right name for me. But this is the only name I know, and I began to write it in its traditional form. I can write 麗 easily, without having to pause to remember if I'm missing a line or a dash or the flick at the end of a tail. It is one of the few dozen Chinese characters I can write and read, tethering me to a country that calls me daughter but that I'm hesitant to call 家.

The artistry behind each character is lost on this page, where they are rendered too straight, too angular, too rigid. What you can't see here is how the stroke order shapes each character, the exact sequence of how each line should be written—left to right, top to bottom, something Holland Christensen's tattoo artist probably did not know.

. . .

My father has a single tattoo. It is the word 忍.

The tattoo was simply native to his body like a limb or organ. I was in my mid-20s when I finally thought to ask him what the character meant; it was not a word we learned in Chinese school.

. . .

When I began this essay, I wanted to show Holland Christensen to herself. I wanted to say, *You made a mistake, and your mistake is my name.* I wanted this white woman to be the proxy, a wall to spit on. I wanted this to be a catharsis, to exorcise a childhood self-consciousness in which I silently thanked my father for giving me an "American" name too so I could be that much closer to whiteness—could know what it felt like to be called something familiar in this country. I wanted her mistake to feel just as debilitating as it had felt to watch a white man lob a slur at my mother and father, who then turned to me to translate. I wanted to point to the hypervisibility of "Chinese" tattoos on non-Chinese bodies versus the invisibility of the Asian diaspora.

I wanted to understand how her mistake had happened and why my idea of catharsis cannot begin and end with her. I wanted to talk to her about how one ends up with a stranger's name permanently inked onto one's body. She agreed to speak with me after I sent her a DM on Twitter and included a link to my website to prove that I was a writer hoping to learn something about her, about myself. So I called her.

• • •

Her friends call her Holly and she lives in Atlanta, where she tried to go to all of the Hawks vs. Nets games until an injury completely sidelined Lin early in the 2017–18 season with the Brooklyn team. (He has since been traded to the Hawks. And Holly is now a season ticket holder.) Before moving to Atlanta, she had lived about an hour south of Salt Lake City, in Orem, Utah. It was in Orem that she printed out three foreign characters and brought them into a tattoo shop.

Ask most people with more than a few tattoos and they'll tell you that at least one of their tattoos was an impulse. Christensen admits she had not done due diligence when she logged on to a language exchange site, where she had been practicing Swedish, and asked for the translation of "My True North." She wanted the phrase in Chinese because, after catching up with a friend who told her about a recent trip to Taiwan, she immediately put the country on a list of vacation destinations.

Her body is home to eight tattoos. Three of them relate to travel, as if they were passport stamps: the Icelandic word *norður* to remember her trip to the Nordic island, a poorly executed outline of the African continent that she admits was a bad idea from her visit to South Africa, and an inspiration to go to Asia for the first time: 林書豪.

A "My True North" tattoo in Chinese made sense to her—it would point her to the island nation thousands of miles away across the Pacific Ocean. I asked a friend who is fluent in Chinese if translation is possible for a phrase like this and he said there isn't a similar idiom in Chinese. But, he said, we could think of the expression to mean, literally, *compass*, 指南豪, which translates to "point south needle." Even if a tattoo that was meant to say "My True North" actually read that it was pointing south, it may have been more fitting, since Christensen was feeling lost.

She got the tattoo days before moving away from Orem, leaving behind a period when she was homebound for months, slogging through a deep depression. In the middle of preparing to move, she had to get out of the house to do something, anything. She needed a "distraction" from her depression. I didn't push her to tell me the specifics of her situation, but she revealed that this Chinese travel tattoo "represented that [she'd] never go to Taiwan because [her] whole life had been destroyed and [she] wasn't planning on being around." She didn't need to explain

> I wanted this white woman to be the proxy, a wall to spit on.

to me any further; I knew that hunger for the sharp vibration of a tattoo machine as a reminder that you're still in a body.

Christensen can't recall who exactly told her the true meaning of her Chinese tattoo. It may have been another person on the language exchange website where she received the inaccurate translation in the first place. Christensen's viral infamy brought on a lot of hate and trolls, but she also made connections and basketball-loving friends. A new life emerged around her mistake. Lin responded to the tattoo with his own post on /r/NBA, linking to a photo of him holding a Sharpie and his Chinese name written on his ankle, with the caption, "Saw this tattoo online and copied it, anyone know what it means?" She even met him, waiting at the players' exit after a game, and he gave her a hug. She said it was a blur. The friend she was with said he smelled really good.

Her mistake gave her something. I was salty about it. But to condemn her for her catharsis would give me absolutely nothing. We spoke for an hour and agreed to catch a Hawks game if I was ever in Atlanta.

· · ·

For some people with Chinese names, the characters that make our names may not merely denote which clan we are from but also show which generation we were born into. Our middle names come from a family poem, with each subsequent generation embodying the next character in the short piece of poetry. Our names mean something; our names are poems.

I, too, went to an internet forum in search of a translation. In the /r/Translator subreddit, I asked for help with my family poem. As a consequence of assimilation, laziness, and Saturday morning Chinese school, my brothers and I never learned beyond very basic Chinese. We can read and write our names, count numbers, and proclaim 我是中國人 (*I am Chinese*). That's about it. I uploaded a photocopy of my father's family poem, one and a half vertical lines of Chinese characters written with a small brush. The longer line is almost the length of a sheet of paper. Nine characters from the top, I recognize the middle name that my brothers and I share: 正, meaning *correct, just, and upright*. Above 正 is my father's middle name: 樹, *tree*.

A stranger on the internet told me that the shorter line merely states that this is the family poem for 林. The longer line is the poem, which roughly translates to:

天大華芳林
The great sky with sweet-smelling flowers in the forest

山輝樹正森
The splendid mountain with upright trees in the woodlands

發生長茂盛
They sprout forth, live, and thrive

永世成佳岑
For all generations in the future, they will complete a beautiful peak of a hill

Our name is a poem about growing so dense we take over a mountainside. Jeremy Lin's middle name is not in my family's poem, but I don't take this to mean we're not related. There's more than one splendid mountain in the range.

. . .

There is a photo of my father at the beach, a few years after he arrived in Southern California from the beaches of Phu Quoc. I remember him wearing only ocean-blue swim trunks, his arms crossed against his bony oak-brown chest, his body lean from neglect, poverty, and a war that I can only imagine. He is the only Chinese person I know who has a Chinese character tattoo that's been earned. It rests on his right deltoid. It's a faded army-green color now, and it is the character for *endure*: 忍.

Endure is a word made up of *knife*: 刀, into the *heart*: 心.

I conjure stories of where he was, who he was with, how he held his arm steady while a friend stuck and poked him during the aftermath of a war. They must have sat on a beach in Phu Quoc, beneath the long shadow of a palm tree at sunset. There must have been a needle, black ink in a small bowl meant for nuoc mam, and his unwashed tanned skin. I think of the stench of body odor, the sheen of hair so dirty that it looked oil-slick clean, and how people were on the verge of tears or had not cried for years. How there was nothing to eat but the heaviness of the humidity in South

Vietnam. It is in these imaginings that I conjure what he endured, what my mother endured, how their endurance led them to endure each other to bring me here.

I texted my father to ask him why *endure*—the tattoo, that is. He replied in English, simply, "Don't have to fight."

I tried to ask him to explain what he meant. But his tattoo is more than ink pierced through his skin—it is a scar. How does one ask her father the origins of a scar without the risk of cutting into it again?

. . .

Every day I log on and scroll through my Instagram feed for the photos of the many tattoo artists I follow. I want to see what's been left indelibly on someone else's body. I zoom in to examine how the line work was done, to contemplate color palettes, how the design fits on a specific limb. It's been a decade since my last tattoo and I'm ready for a few more. Been thinking about dogwoods and magnolias for years.

Lately I've been searching #hongkongtattoos to see what the shops and artists are doing in that small island country. The territory of China is home to a population of Vietnamese refugees, many of whom are of Chinese ancestry. I relish seeing Chinese character tattoos on Chinese bodies by Chinese artists. Perhaps my own true north will point me to Hong Kong, where I can trust that they'll give me my father's tattoo of a knife in a heart—a way to show that I, too, survived something. 🖋

FUCK YOU BOB DYLAN THIS ONE IS MINE
or BLACK SNAKE

Fuck you, Bob Dylan, I ain't
sleeping through this
gorgeous storm.

The angry eye of Pocahontas
peeks at me from a bucket
because the buffalo of North
Dakota need me to speak of
their civil disobediences,

Black Snake's going down.

So let me let this skid-row
prophet announce the second
Saturday of ever,

Black Snake's going down.

I haven't prayed in days
so everything I say must be
a prayer,
everything I do an
exaltation of the Lord who lives
in my cat claws.

Black Snake's going down.

Loving anything is painful,
even especially God will shatter
your beloved eyeballs
like a windshield
in a hurricane of hockey sticks
until you know
you don't need no eyes
to understand the buffalo bleeds
about bigger things
and Marlon Brando was a buffalo.

IF BY TORCH

If by torch you mean flashlight then
yes, I carry that and I flick it off
and on so maybe it's a lighter, a
Bic flickering in the fickle wind of
my whims. I only know I don't want to
talk about it when Thalia gets on the
R train at Prospect Avenue and sits
down next to me, it's 8:48, I'm
going to be late, no matter that I'd
rather be on the back of a Vespa
buzzing across the antique lace bridge
and off into the pleasures of the night,
it's morning and I have a date with the
snow-blank page. Thalia sitting next to me
says in a voice full of clicks that is just
a whisper, "Write about the butterfly"
she means the one that flew into my mouth
Wednesday when the blue yolk of an eye hit
mine, shook my hand and took me all apart.
I'm trying to hold my shit together with
hairpins and a blue bandana but such
feelings, so fine, lack volume, lack body,
slip out greasy, making me look crazy

undone and nauseous with this butterfly
fluttering in my gut, my torch beam burns
bright, my lighter my Bic is flicked and I
want to tell Thalia that my muse must be
a man and she tells me in her voice full
of clicks, just a whisper that she is the
mother of every man that inspired me
before, they've all been as real as that so
I ask her, "Even the ones I fucked?"

Preservation

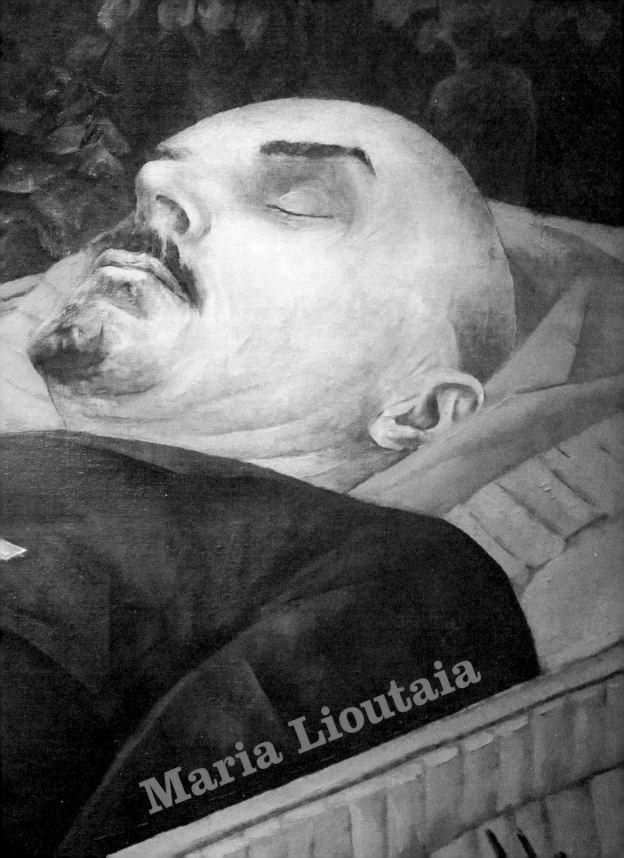

Over the past month, Valentina had attempted every procedure, from reputable to highly experimental. She'd bathed Lenin's body in hydrogen peroxide and potassium acetate, employed benzene wipes, adjusted the dosages of intravenous polymer, applied refined paraffin wax in a thin layer over the face to maintain the appearance of skin, even resorted to botulinum. But the corpse had ceased all cooperation. After seventy years of successful maintenance, Lenin's body was deteriorating faster than the morticians and biochemical scientists could keep up. Patchy dark spots bloomed across the dome of Lenin's skull. His eye sockets collapsed like sinkholes. That morning, as Valentina inspected a gray fleshy protrusion on his temple, his left ear had fallen off into her hand like the handle on a poorly made clay mug. Most worryingly, there was a new smell about him. A damp, ghoulish, subterranean stench.

Valentina took the creaking elevator from her basement office at the Red Square mausoleum to the viewing chamber, where she could peek into the main room through brocade velvet curtains. Lenin was arranged on the central dais, as always, strategically spotlit by a soft peach wash over his recessed features. Today he was dressed in a black wool suit with double lapels and a maroon pinstripe tie. They'd had to change his suits almost daily this week, to keep up with his skin secretions. His face was serene, as though he were simply indulging in closed-eyed contemplation after a busy day of guiding the proletariat. Despite the flattering shadows of the room, Valentina could see the cluster of fungus on his bald pate through the glut of concealer.

The bare-headed procession of schoolchildren, pensioners, and tourists shuffled by on a cordoned walkway. Attendance had noticeably declined in the past year, since the dissolution of the USSR. For most visitors, dead Lenin was now just a morbid curiosity, one more thing off the Red Square checklist, after buying ice cream *plombir* at GUM and a photo with a celebrity impersonator. Biting editorials in the newspapers suggested that Lenin should be put to real rest, buried in the Kremlin's walls so the country could move on into a post-Soviet future without its history so prominently on display. Valentina listened to the hush, the whisper of feet on carpet, watched the shadow-chiseled faces passing under the peach light. And in the middle of it all Lenin, glowing on the dais, magnetizing attention toward himself, the epicenter of their gaze.

Most people thought of death as an instant: a transition from being to not-being, like flipping a light switch. But Valentina understood it as a progressive condition everyone was born with, a deterioration that was irrevocably intertwined with life. Cellular degradation began long before—and continued long after—the ceasing of the heartbeat. To be able to contain the process this long, to keep Lenin's body looking nearly alive, felt almost like commanding time itself.

> Most worryingly, there was a new smell about him. A damp, ghoulish, subterranean stench.

Valentina savored, too, the intimacy of knowing someone after death. Her relationship with Lenin had exceeded her marriage. She knew that pale, waxy body better than her ex-husband's and better than her son's. Living bodies changed constantly. Acquiring new moles and stretch marks, growing hirsute or bald, wracked with new aches and smells and destructive bad habits. The encroachment of menopause was rendering Valentina's own body alien, from the hot flashes that left hives under the folds of her breasts, to the relaxation of her jawline, its slow sag. Some mornings she looked down in the shower and barely recognized the landscape.

Lenin's body, on the other hand, had been comfortingly consistent. Valentina had memorized the mole constellation on his back, the soft skin valleys between his ribs, the gaping maw of his abdominal incision, how the wiry bristle of his copper chest hair felt across her palm. But now he, too, was changing, rejecting all attempts to preserve him.

Valentina watched as each person came level with Lenin's head: their chins lifted, eyes flickered at the body in nervous confusion, nostrils flared. That dendritic smell threaded itself through the room and announced with certainty that Lenin was decomposing.

"Valentina Nikolaevna, phone for you downstairs," said Katya at her back.

As Valentina stepped off the elevator, Boris walked by with a stack of fresh gauze, trailing the smell of formaldehyde down the hallway. She entered her windowless office, lowered herself into the chair, brought the receiver to her ear.

"Valentinushka, how's Comrade Lenin? Back to tip-top shape?" It was Anton Antonovich Saratin, the director of the Institute of Cultural Preservation.

Valentina twisted her fingers into the telephone cord. "Unfortunately, he's not cooperating just yet."

There was a pause at the other end. A long pause.

> Lenin rested supine and naked on a metal table under UV lamps.

"Well, make him—I just had word that the Ministry of Culture is sending an inspector tomorrow morning, since there's been some public reports of a rotting stench. And do you know what will happen if they find him ready for burial? *Kaput*, that's what. For all of you down there. Possibly for me as well."

Under her sternum, Valentina felt the sprouting of panic. "I need more time."

A sigh on his end, the scrape of a heavy chair against wooden floorboards. "I don't care what you have to do, shove Plasticine up his ass, lacquer him with nail polish, just make him look presentable tomorrow." And there was the dial tone in Valentina's ear.

She sat for a long time staring at objects on her desk—a pen, a conjoined tail of paper clips, a little figurine of a knight constructed out of acorns, twigs, and prodigious blobs of glue that Yurik had made in school years ago. What could be done? They'd already tried everything within budget and scientific reason. Could they make a wax figure of Lenin to temporarily replace the body? This required expertise, carvers and painters they didn't have on staff and wouldn't have been able to pay anyway. Plus, there was the issue of time. A wax copy would take time, and she had fewer than twenty-four hours at her disposal. There was really nothing to do. She'd already failed.

"Katya, get everyone in here," she called into the hallway.

The half-dozen mausoleum staff made their way into her office, and Valentina glanced around in preemptive farewell. Her long-suffering ficus plant, its leaves in need of dusting. A gold tinsel garland pinned over her doorway and a miniature plastic fir tree decorated with tiny baubles in a ceramic pot on the corner of her desk. Two days before New Year's. And now Valentina had to announce that Grandfather Frost was bringing everyone unemployment.

She explained the situation, but didn't have to explain the impossibility of passing the inspection.

"Is there nothing we can do?" said Boris, leaning against the doorframe, a smear of something brown and Lenin down the lapel of his lab coat.

"What, dress you up as him and hope for the best?" fired someone from the back, and there was a dry chuckle, followed by resigned silence.

Valentina looked at all of them. "There's no use you being here tomorrow for the inspection. Go home early, try to enjoy the New Year's holidays, and may '93 be kinder to us all."

They closed the mausoleum early, removed Lenin from display into the laboratory downstairs. Her colleagues stopped by her office one by one to shake her hand and wish her happy New Year in mournful tones, before departing. Even Boris left eventually, after attempting final, futile attempts at resurrection. Then she was alone. She ripped the gold tinsel down from the doorway and wrapped it around the acorn knight before tucking the figurine into her purse. She wasn't sure if the ficus plant counted as government property, so didn't risk taking it. She put on her raccoon-fur coat, picked up her bags, locked her office, and walked down the hallway to the refrigerated laboratory.

Lenin rested supine and naked on a metal table under UV lamps, a square of quinine-soaked gauze plastered onto his forehead. There were new gray striations along the veins of his feet, and his skin looked like old tights: too taut and threadbare in some regions, too loose and wrinkled in others.

Valentina stood over him a long time, then took his cold, stiff hand in hers and said, "Traitor," before bursting into tears.

She tied her wool scarf around her head and gathered the collar of her coat tight to her neck against the bluster of damp wind racing across the expanse of Red Square. A blind sun smeared low across the sky, and the clouds on the horizon were leaden with coming snow. On the front steps of the mausoleum, Valentina rearranged her bags into the crook of her arm, ducked her head low in the wind, and took a diagonal direction past

Saint Basil's. She had no particular destination in mind. It felt too early to go home. The cobblestones under her boots were slick with gray slush.

Her wedding portraits had been taken not far from where she walked now. On the other side of the square, in front of the Eternal Flame. The memory was more painful than tender. The Moskvich auto-body factory where Alexei had worked for a decade had closed three years ago, and he'd started moonlighting in small garages, where vodka and despair were ever present. The verb *spilsya* had always intrigued Valentina with its accuracy. It implied not just drunkenness, but a concluded descent into drunkenness, as though taking regularly to the bottle was a slide covered in noxious slime, with no way back up. It implied a process, a degradation of will and faculties and resistance. She'd tried begging, coaxing, threatening. She'd tried hiding the money, but while she was at work Alexei hawked her jewelry and her father's photographic equipment at bazaars for a fraction of their worth. She'd brought him to countless specialists, including a hypnotist in the suburbs. She'd even bribed an old school friend—now a doctor in a government hospital—for a referral to the high-end sanatorium in the invigorating pinewoods north of Moscow. Alexei spent two weeks there, then the day after returning home fell off their third-floor balcony drunk and broke his collarbone. Once the sling came off, Valentina told him to leave, for their son's sake more than for her own.

This square held nothing but reminders of how things altered cruelly and permanently. Her life was in its autumn, lonely and losing leaves. Valentina made it to the fir alleyway that ran parallel to the Kremlin's wall, where wide-backed benches stood at intervals along the walkway, though most were damp with snowmelt or tagged with loopy graffiti. She walked until she found one sufficiently protected by a sprawling blue fir and cleaner than the others. A man behind an issue of *Pravda* occupied one end. Valentina wiped the slats on the other end with her handkerchief, then sat down.

The day was quickly withering. People hurried toward the metro to beat the rush hour, here and there impersonators walked about alone or in pairs looking for tourists to take a photo with them for a couple of rubles. There were a few Stalins, a Marx or two, a random smattering of Pushkins and Tolstoys, but the majority were Lenins with varying degrees of physical resemblance and comportment. How dare they presume to look like him, thought Valentina. It was, in fact, hard to pick the worst resemblance. Perhaps the gangly Lenin trying to light a cigarette in the wind, his too-short army-issue pants showing hairy ankles. Or the one barely in his midtwenties, hiding his full head of curls under a cap. Posing with a young couple in front of a Kremlin wall was a doughy Lenin with the red-veined potato nose and under-eye paunchiness of a committed alcoholic. Worthless imitations, the lot of them.

Valentina heard an "Excuse me" and glanced up. But the woman holding a small boy by the hand wasn't talking to her. She was addressing the man with the *Pravda* on the other end of Valentina's bench. "Excuse me, could we take a picture with you?"

The woman gestured vaguely at her son, who sucked on a mittened hand. The man on the bench slowly and carefully started folding his newspaper, and Valentina realized that he was another Lenin impersonator, with a black overcoat open to a slightly bulging vest. Before Valentina could take a good look, the woman extended to her a boxy chrome-and-black Zenit. "Could I ask you to take the photograph, please? Do you know how to work a camera?"

> **As the Lenin's features sharpened, a surreal prickling of recognition made Valentina freeze.**

Valentina nodded. Her father had taught her, and she'd taken all of their family snapshots herself, developed them in the bathroom, before Alexei had sold the camera and lenses.

She took a few steps away as the Lenin stood and mother and son posed stiffly beside him. She pressed her right eye against the viewfinder and twisted the lens, bringing the scene into focus. As the Lenin's features sharpened, a surreal prickling of recognition made Valentina freeze. Something about the way he held himself, stiff but commanding. The carefully trimmed mustache and ruddy beard framing that familiar thin-lipped mouth. That sharp ridge of cheekbone. And those eyes, with their almost Asiatic narrowing in the corners.

She lowered the camera.

"Did you take it?" the woman called.

Valentina lifted the camera once more, wound up the film, counted out loud, "One, two, three," heard the snap of the shutter, and handed the Zenit back to the woman, all in a haze.

The woman extended a handful of coins, asking the impersonator, "Is this enough?" He nodded curtly, then dropped the change into his overcoat pocket with a little pat. Then he sat back onto the bench and raised the *Pravda* back up to his face.

Valentina waited until the mother and son were far away. The only thing she could make out beyond the open swath of newsprint was the man's left ear—small, delicately sculpted, with a defined and well-curved rim, an ear that was painfully familiar to her after she'd spent the past week trying to get it to stay on Lenin's head. Valentina felt a kaleidoscoping of reality that made her clutch the bench slats to offset a sudden swirl of dizziness.

After a couple of moments she finally found her voice. "Pardon me, comrade?"

Sergey looked up at the Kremlin's walls as though there were still snipers positioned at the embrasures.

The Lenin tipped one corner of the newspaper and faced her. It really was uncanny. The only thing that allowed Valentina to be sure was the eye color. Lenin's eyes had been dark brown, almost black. Beady. Those who'd seen them in person said that gaze perforated their thoughts, left gashes for his ideas to blow through. This Lenin had eyes of warm honey, amber-sealed, kind and tired.

"It's incredible," Valentina murmured. "Are you by any chance related?"

It would've been a ridiculous question even a few years ago, Lenin's relative busking for change on Red Square, but was a reasonable possibility in the present confusion. Chemists were quitting broke universities for open-air market stands, mathematicians added spare cash as gypsy cabbies, policemen supplemented their income in the employ of mobsters.

Only after she spoke did Valentina realize she hadn't specified whom she meant, but by the definitive shake of this Lenin's head, it was evident she didn't need to.

His face darkened. "Devil take it all, no. A genetic curse, a cosmic joke." He spat on the ground as if he'd bitten into lemon peel.

The vehemence was so pronounced, Valentina drew back. "Is it really so terrible?"

He looked at her for a long silent moment, and Valentina felt herself blushing.

"You have no idea, believe me. Did you want a photo, too?"

"Not quite," whispered Valentina.

She explained to this Lenin—his name was Sergey—the plan that had formed at her first glance of him. Once he understood what she was asking of him, he bolted up from the bench. But instead of leaving, he began pacing back and forth under the fir trees along the pavement, folding and unfolding his newspaper, flushed pink continents materializing on his forehead. On the one hand the risk of being found out, arrested, charged with—what? Surely not treason. Tampering with a dead body? Valentina wasn't sure what the charge would be, save there would be one if they were caught. On the other hand, his overcoat was threadbare in the elbows, his shoes scuffed and thin-soled. He stopped sharply in front of Valentina and asked, his eyes downcast to the cobblestones, "So, say I do. How much?"

Valentina offered the entirety of her week's salary. She and Yurik would get by, and a successful inspection could buy time. Maybe over the holidays she would figure out how to restore the real Lenin back to normal.

Sergey looked up at the Kremlin's walls as though there were still snipers positioned at the embrasures. He kept rubbing his head, smoothing his hand down toward his face. Then he looked at Valentina again, carefully and steadily, for so long she became suddenly aware of her puffy post-cry nose, the fine lines around her mouth, the gray starting to show at the roots of her brunette bob. He nodded.

Valentina had little memory of how she got home. The press of silent bodies in the train car, the looming of her apartment building in the swirl of snow, her hand trembling so much that the key scraped against the metal of the lock before finding the keyhole. The apartment was silent. Only the quiet ticking of the stove clock and the muted shouts of the neighbors' television. A scrawled note slipped under a dirty plate on the kitchen table informing her in Yurik's disheveled handwriting that he was studying tonight at Dima's. She drew one finger through the remnants of strawberry compote on the plate. She felt she was operating in some ether, the ether of dread of the next day.

Valentina moved over to perch on the windowsill, then drew the telephone into her lap. She picked and pulled at the numbers one by one, the rotary disk clicking back with each circumnavigation of the dial. She took a deep steadying breath.

"Oh, Annechka, you're still at work, good." Annechka was one of her oldest friends, a veterinarian. "Listen, I need a big favor. My cousin, she's got this dog to transport from Lithuania, a guard dog, and it's not exactly an aboveground transportation, if you know what I mean. They've got to keep him completely quiet in the truck over the border. Is there something they can give him, to make him stay asleep for a couple of hours? One of those big drooling beasties, with the thick coat. A Caucasian Ovcharka, yes. Oh, I'd say—" Valentina had lifted embalmed Lenin's body often, but it was a different matter when it was full of blood and organs. Miscalculation could be deadly. "I'd say around seventy-five, eighty kilos. Yes"—she laughed—"a big one. They're willing to pay, you understand, more than the usual rate." Valentina glanced at the small soup tureen stored on top of the fridge, where she'd hidden some sparse savings meant for Yurik's new winter boots and perhaps eventually a Black Sea vacation for herself. "Oh, Annechka, I'll pop over right now. You're a lifesaver."

She couldn't fall asleep. Headlights from passing cars chased each other across the ceiling and twice she got up to check that the vial was still in her coat pocket. Around midnight she heard the soft click of the door latch as Yurik snuck in well past his curfew, the stumbling and quiet swearing as he tripped taking off his shoes in the hallway, the gurgle of urine hitting the toilet bowl, the creak of the foldout couch springs in the other room. Now an adolescent, he seemed too tall and angular for their cramped apartment. The first time his voice had broken, Valentina was so startled by the man's timbre that came out of her small son that she dropped the pot of water she'd been carrying to the stove. Just yesterday she'd caught him smoking near the building entrance. As she'd swatted him upstairs, he walked slowly, with a new swagger, something insolent and foreign in his eyes. By dinnertime he was back to himself, but that insight into her son as no longer her child had terrified Valentina.

At five, she gave up on sleep and headed to the mausoleum. She spent the early hours packing up Lenin's body. He looked worse than the previous day. The gray striations now threaded over his thighs and up to his groin, as though time were collecting him in monstrous tentacles. Before zipping him up in a white bag and sliding him into the storage pod, she leaned down and pressed her lips hard against his cold, damp forehead.

"Where do you want me?" Sergey stood awkwardly in front of the dais, hands shoved deeply into the pockets of his navy tracksuit.

"First, change into this," Valentina said, handing him one of Lenin's black suits along with a white shirt and striped gray tie. It was a suit they hadn't used in the rotation in a while, and it had been cleaned, but it still emanated subtle pickle-like notes of fermentation.

Sergey drew his hand across the wool, slightly frowning. Then he flipped up the manufacturer tag of the suit and laughed a short sad bark of a sound.

"I made this suit," he said.

Valentina didn't understand.

"You think I've been busking on the Red Square my whole life?" He fingered the suit collar. "I used to have a real job. Supervisor of production at the wool factory in Yekaterinburg."

"So why did you leave?" Valentina asked.

Sergey sighed. "I was liquidated ten months ago. The official cause was the plant's restructuring, but an old colleague higher up told me the real one. They'd determined that, for the purposes of proceeding into a post-Soviet future, it wouldn't do to have such a walking, talking, daily reminder of the old guard. In a managerial role, even." He chuckled.

> "I drive a cab at night. The drunks think they've got delirium tremens when they see me."

"I tried finding another job, but everyone took one look at me and doubled over laughing, sent someone to find a camera for a quick snap with their arm around the great man's shoulders before telling me the position's already been filled. What else can I do? I'm alone, no parents, no wife, so I come to Moscow. I drive a cab at night. The drunks think they've got delirium tremens when they see me. Who'd believe it was Lenin giving them a lift? Who needs a Lenin in these times?" He shrugged.

"I do," Valentina said, and he looked up at her with those warm brown eyes. Valentina was the first to break their gaze. "Now, change."

She ducked behind the brocade curtains, but instead of turning away, found herself compelled to watch. She gripped the velvet and leaned into a crack between the fabric. Sergey inspected the stack of clothing in his hands, rotated it slowly, then placed it on the dais and unzipped his sweat suit. Valentina had been expecting to see that familiar body, waxy and dessicated, so Sergey's pale manly vigor sent a bolt through her. Yes, there was that ruddy chest hair, which made her palm tingle in recognition, the bare feet she knew so well flexing against the carpet. But this body was whole, living, pulsing with life and blood. Watching the muscles shift under his skin as he bent down to pull off his slacks made Valentina's breath run shallow. This feeling brought a new awareness to her body, a trembling that made her heated with shame.

When Sergey finished dressing, she waited before slipping back through the curtains. The suit fit as if it were made for him, which she supposed it was.

"I need you to climb up here." Valentina nodded at the empty black silken indentation where real-Lenin had lain just a day ago. Sergey eyed it reluctantly, then, hiking up his pant leg, he hoisted himself onto the raised platform. Valentina began arranging the heavy brocade covering over his feet up to his waist, as she used to tuck Yurik in at night, except here she was tucking in Lenin to his final rest, making him nice and dead again. Sergey lay still as she tweaked his collar and tie, arranged his hands in position on his thighs. His hands were warm and dry, making a comforting papery sound against her own skin. As Valentina smoothed back the hair on the side of his head, Sergey closed his eyes.

> But living bodies were deceptive, they changed. She imagined Sergey fatter, balder.

"Would you like to hear a joke?" he asked her. She expected some variant on *a German, an American, and a Russian are shipwrecked on a desert island*, but Sergey said,

"How do you describe all of Russian history in just one sentence?"

Valentina shrugged.

"And then it got worse," he said.

She reached down into her bag and laid out the syringe, a bottle of rubbing alcohol and cotton balls, the small glass vial of cloudy liquid. "I'm going to give you the sedative now," she said. She couldn't decide whether Sergey's agreement to the plan was a sign of immoderate optimism or terminal pessimism. Considering his life, she guessed the latter. Valentina inserted the syringe into the vial's rubber stopper, flipped it upside down, drew back the plunger. The liquid swirled in hypnotic tendrils.

"Don't worry," she said, pulling up the sleeve of his suit and rubbing down the bulging vein in the crook of his arm with an alcohol-soaked cotton ball. "I'm basically a doctor."

He was looking up at her with an expression she couldn't decipher. As she touched the needle to his skin, he quickly placed a pausing, callused hand on hers.

"Say, after this," he said, so quietly that she had to lean in close to hear, "would you want to get some tea with me? Maybe catch a play?" He looked more nervous about her reply than the needle. Maybe she had him pegged wrong, she thought as she stared at him in confusion, as she stabbed the needle into his arm, as she pushed the plunger. Maybe he was, after all, an optimist.

"Okay," she said, as his breathing deepened, the eyelids coming down like stage curtains, and there was Lenin proper in front of her, motionless and serene.

It was a possibility that hadn't occurred to her, despite the heat she'd felt watching him get undressed. A life with Lenin, outside the mausoleum. But living bodies were deceptive, they changed. She imagined Sergey fatter, balder. Sergey, taken to drink. Having to watch him grow older than Lenin, deteriorate in real life. And here he was now, so trusting, so perfect, just her and Lenin's body in the cocooning silence of the mausoleum. Dust swirled through shafts of soft electric light, and everything felt right again.

Valentina's hands reached to arrange the silken pillow beneath his head. Then her hands slipped the pillow out from under him, gently, gently, laying his head back against the dais. And then her hands hovered the pillow over his face, brushed his skin with the black silk, stroked his face with it like a mother would touch the face of her newborn. That was another possibility, right there, and she found herself surprised that she was capable of it. Her hands placed the pillow lightly against his mouth and nose, then lifted it again after a moment, like a bee alighting on a flower. It was as if the universe had brought her this Lenin as a replacement for the old one, as a way of restarting, of trying again. The staff would come in after New Year's and she would tell them, a miracle, comrades! I have solved it, I solved it for all of us. Everything is exactly as it was before. A deteriorated body could be disposed, there were ways of doing that. In this troubled time, many people went missing, and who would look for him? He had said it himself: no parents, no wife. If anyone did search for him, they wouldn't suspect the body that'd been lying there for seventy years, observed by hundreds of people a day.

What loneliness it was, to choose.

"Statute four hundred and ninety two, Valentina Nikolaevna, deterioration of cultural relics, this is a serious allegation," sighed the inspector from the Ministry of Culture, removing his fur hat and placing it on a ledge by the door. A sparse comb-over of white hair gleamed wetly in the dim light. "This isn't how it used to be, you know. Everything used to be proper, by-the-book. Culture was respected, but now it's all pell-mell, now who can tell what's going on? It's not polite, to have Vladimir Ilyich rotting and out on display, just not polite."

"Goodness, who is rotting?" said Valentina, trying to keep her breathing deep and even. She smiled pleasantly. "A small skin fungus we didn't catch in time, and someone noticed. We dealt with it promptly. Properly. Come, see for yourself." She extended her arm like a tour guide to indicate the body on the dais.

The inspector straightened his jacket, cleared his throat, smoothed his hair. He ascended the two steps with difficulty, leaning on his cane. Valentina stood shoulder to shoulder with him, looking down at Sergey's face.

"See," said Valentina. "He's no worse for wear."

"My lights," the inspector coughed. "He really does look quite lifelike. Quite lifelike indeed." He leaned in. "You've done a tremendous job. Why, he looks like he just died yesterday." He reached out a hand slowly, as though hypnotized. As his hand descended reverently toward Sergey's face, in that gesture Valentina recognized a man unmoored, reaching toward a familiar past he could not admit he missed.

She quickly put a firm hand on his sleeve, catching his fingers just before touchdown. "Please, do refrain from touching. We suspect the fungal infection came from unprotected contact." She knew that even an old, fumbling man would be able to tell the difference between a warm, pliant body and one dead for seventy years.

"Of course, of course. Protocol. Well done." He wiped his hand on his trousers, then continued to stare down at Lenin's face.

"Well," he said finally. "Well." Valentina heard a faint tremor in his voice and wanted to tell him, It will be okay. Maybe this time it won't get worse.

The inspector cleared his throat. "No matter. I will confirm with the ministry that Comrade Lenin is as spry as ever. God grant such good health to us all."

They shook hands at the door. He backed out of the room, wishing her a happy New Year, his gaze on Lenin to the last.

As the inspector left, it seemed to Valentina that he took all sound with him. There was a ringing in her ears. Valentina turned slowly toward the dais. Sergey's profile glowed serene and heartbreakingly beautiful. She began to walk across the room back to him, every movement caught in thick light. Her shoes rustled against the carpet, the room swallowing sound. As she walked, a strange fear began to unfurl inside her at the sight of the perfectly still body on the dais, and the air transmuted. Reality became suspended, sealed in amber. Time trembled, a tangible curtain she could brush aside and walk through, and the body on the dais was no longer Sergey as Lenin, but Lenin himself, Lenin as he had recently died, so recently that no one except Valentina knew about it yet, or else Lenin as he had not yet died, as no one except Valentina knew he was going to die. As if she had finally succeeded in truly pausing time, preventing anything from ever changing. She sank down on the carpet, her back against the dais, and closed her eyes. She sat like that for what felt like minutes, hours. Finally, she heard a ragged inhale above her, a soft moan. She stood up, bent over Sergey, and touched his face. He slowly opened his eyes. Then he smiled, and it was the guileless, drug-drunken smile of Sergey completely, not of Lenin at all, and Valentina found that she liked it quite a lot. She brought her lips to his face, kissing his wide forehead, trailing her mouth down to the contours of his thin, pliant lips.

The inspector from the Ministry of Culture stood in the doorway of the viewing chamber, clutching the fur hat he'd forgotten and returned for, and watching Valentina and the corpse of Lenin hold each other tenderly under the shimmering peach lighting streaming down like heavenly approbation. Tears etched his lined face. For the rest of his life, the inspector never told anyone about the impossible moment he was witness to. On his deathbed six years later, the final crackling gasp of his mind recalled the image of Valentina's reverently closed eyes as Lenin lifted a hand and softly cupped it against her cheek. 🔯

Mai Der Vang

AUTHORIZATION TO DEPART RAVAGED HOMELAND AS BIOMEDICAL SAMPLE

flew you afar piecemealed
bits of spleen liver tissues of the second
 gut orphaned by the whole
    routed you in a vacutainer ||
bangkok | frankfurt delayed | dulles | fort detrick
  as if only born to serve in
      postmortem   detain offerings of
cerebral shards to be juried under a lens
    flew you | from the silken
  wilderness | of | your | viscera
        from all   the   vacated
   leftovers of yourself   sinews snipped |
culled from the ribs | in this   mission of guilt for
  your un-leaving you've trekked
far from the village   salvaged in | sides   from you
     and other hundreds   sealed on letter | head
  dispersed to the globe | here at long last in these united
          states   you did not land a body
    only | as a vial of blood | were you registered
    as urine   did they label you : asylum

sample M-35-82 | victim "7" en
route to london
fluids of you granted fare to
enter refugee airspace
while ending away in hospital camp
stayed behind the | sourced | you
and every
else
part

sample M-25-82 victim "9"
no weekend courier ambiguously arriving
so stomach of laments

||||| *how could they not*
get you here somehow
only drops
relayed: lab to: lab | to: lab
cargo of you | quaking inside
an ice chest

MYTH

after Yusef Komunyakaa

Say we do become more heat than body. Say
    a creek burning silver in midsummer, a boy
in a tree or a boy learning the taste of pebbles.
    Say the bird shelved away like porcelain,
porcelain spent for harvest. Sheathed light
    cheapened for purchase. Say *September*
is the name of my father. Say my father
    buries dolls in the hunting ground, steeps
a prayer in broth & jasmine. Say a wound
    licked clean. Say the green that I crafted
from your hands. The lighthouse with my voice.
    The lighthouse we lived in until the mail
arrived from overseas. As if we knew
    something more about language, the shape
of our names in the mother tongue. We forget
    how to swim. In the film where we live
underwater, you eat black beans in sunlight
    & I tape postcards to the moon.
We found it lodged in the cliff, wrapped it
    in tinfoil. Used it for shelter at night. This,
a body I could say was mine to occupy.

Yes, I could say that this was how I learned
to unfreeze ice, breathe fire, draw maps
   teeming with skin. Says my father, sleeping
under floorboards with feathers for warmth.
   As close to hibernation as anyone could get.
Says the lighthouse at dusk. Says the shadow
   that walked off with my body.

AUGUST STORY

It begins with you building that glass house
from the sky down in the coastal town
where I ruined my voice into song. A string

of fish. A pagoda with no windows. A forest
threaded over ocean. Another day spent
wishing away shell casings & broken earth.

Another day spent in dark rooms & stage lights,
playing fiction. This could have been the story
where I discover a better use for the blood

in my mouth. This could still be that story.
Up close, your eyes look so much darker.
August mists around our teeth & the air

clears when we speak. The story begins
with purple forests & punched-out lights.
The old glory. Open theater in the ravine

where I transform into bushfire at the sound
of applause. I know how to play my audience.
I know how you've always liked birds, their colors

in laughter. It is August & I've run out
of things to say, ways to begin. The storm
I weaned off newspaper headlines.

The storm with my blood on its hands.

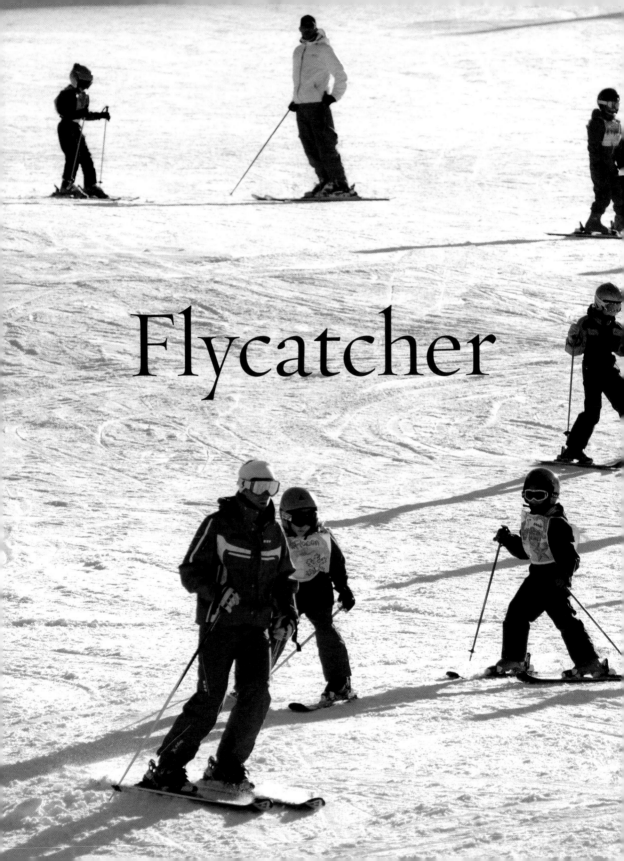

Flycatcher

FICTION

Aleksandar Hemon

I

WE WOULD TAKE A TRAIN TO PAZARIC, THEN MARCH UP THE mountain for a long time. I don't remember the details of that march, except that I was panting and sweating, probably because of the altitude, maybe apprehension. We might've carried our backpacks, but we didn't carry our skis, yet they would arrive with our suitcases in the Šavnici mountain lodge; someone took care of the things outside our purview, made the world work. I wasn't a good skier then—I was nine and a half— and I hated mountaineering, which was walking either uphill or downhill, neither direction enjoyable, and was often cold. In short, I dreaded going to the lodge, but my parents and their friends had all decided to send their children away to the Bjelašnica mountain for the winter break. They had plans for us, hopes to expose us to the varieties of the world and make us better people. The plan would in the long run fail terribly, not because of us or our parents, but because the world is the totality of facts and not of things, let alone intentions. Still, there I was, up in the goddamn mountain all by myself. The children of my parents' friends were all a bit older and thoroughly ignored me as soon we were out of our parents' sight. I shared a room with seven other boys; as the youngest among them, I was given the worst bed—an upper bunk right by a drafty window, the intricate handiwork of ice on its pane. The oldest boy—a tall eighth-grader—was the room leader. I don't remember his name, but I remember his pubescent reek and square jaw and nocturnal noises, which disgusted me and would lead to even more disgusting experiments on my part. He didn't like me, and neither did the other boys, who quickly figured out the advantages of and rewards for their proximity and obedience to the square-jawed leader. I was at the bottom of the hierarchy, which wasn't my natural

ALEKSANDAR HEMON

position—in my normal life, in my school, at the foot of the mountain, so to speak, I wasn't trampled upon. The mountain was a different setup; in this high-altitude winter camp there were no school or street friends, nobody who appreciated my jokes, who knew I was smart, who had a crush on me. My roommates bullied me, teased me, made fun of the way I skied; of my uncouth wooden skis; of my laced boots, peasant-knitted wool mittens, and pom-pom cap. The leader's job was to make sure the room was all clean and neat, and he'd give me orders to straighten up the beds or sweep the floor, which I defiantly ignored. When I wasn't forced to ski, I spent time reading, which was weird to them, and catching flies, which was even weirder. The flies would hibernate in suspended animation when the lodge was unheated, but they would awake after it warmed up and get excited as though God had changed His mind and suddenly granted them eternal summer. Lying in my bed, I'd watch the doomed flies bump against the window pane, buzzing as if trying to cut it with a minuscule circular saw, unable to escape, unaware that they would

I remember his pubescent reek and square jaw and nocturnal noises, which disgusted me.

in fact die if they did. I'd scoop them with a lightning forehand, one or two at a time—though my personal record was seven—then imprison them in a jar, where they would continue to run hopelessly their tiny saws. What is this biological desire for freedom? There are no grounds for believing that the simplest eventuality will in fact be realized. These flies were slow because they were coming out of hibernation, returning from their afterlife, so to speak. Sometimes, I'd pour water over them and drown them all. As flies to wanton boys, so they were to me; I killed them for my sport. That winter, in the two weeks in the Šavnici mountain lodge, I caught dozens, practically every foolish fly that ever made the mistake of entering my room and pressing its feeble saw against my window. Nevertheless, being a Flycatcher could never be interpreted as flattering: my vile roommates readily deployed the new moniker for debasing me in front of others, for mocking me before an audience of girls. I'd considered my female mountaineer comrades on our way up the mountain, and kept a hope burning I could spend some time with at least one of them, alone, talking—talking was my forte. Earning the title of Flycatcher, however, extinguished even the feeblest of flames, yet there was also a liberation from the heavy chains of hope: now I could just keep doing what I liked to do, what I was good at, and not give a flying fuck. The more flies I captured and executed, the more my roommates despised me, not only because flycatching was repulsive, but also because they hated the staunch efficacy of my defiance. Their bullying never made me cry or yearn to be one of them. I just killed the fucking flies and read, devouring chocolate rum bars I spent all my money on at the cafeteria. It drove those boys crazy that they couldn't really touch me, that my flies and I were beyond their reach; it pissed them off so much that one day they planted an icicle in my bed, which I discovered when I lay down on it. It took me a moment to process the sensory information—a sharp, painful cold against my ass—while my roommates giggled, turned on by their deed. I jumped off the bunk, shoved aside the boy who dutifully stepped in front of me, went straight to the room where the grown-up counselors were getting drunk on rum-laced tea, and reported the egregious act. I was angry then, as I am now, not so much because they bullied or insulted me, but because they didn't know me, the true me, they never heard what I could say, what I thought. They deemed me stupid and weak because they didn't know what was inside me—back then a warm ocean, now this vast frozen sea—and they didn't give a damn. The world of a happy boy is a different one from that of an unhappy boy. The grown-up counselor, whose mountain sunburned face I can presently picture, but whose name has always been unknown to me, summoned the boys for a makeshift interrogation. He sternly demanded the facts of the case from them. They stared at the tea-splattered floor, occasionally glancing with hatred at me, who faced them all alone; the room leader confirmed that a large icicle had indeed been planted in the plaintiff's bunk, while insisting he'd known nothing about it. Whereupon the counselor dressed down the boys for betraying their fellow mountaineer, thus betraying the very spirit of the mountain, where everyone should stand for one another and help them in difficulty and adversity, dig them out of an avalanche if need be. Pointing at me, he said, He is your *comrade*! Compelled to look at me, they saw the exact opposite of a comrade. They didn't dare show how much they hated me, but I knew very well. I wasn't their comrade, nor could I ever be—I was Flycatcher, and they were idiots, committed bullies, and masturbators—but I savored their being humiliated, relished the fact that I was now under higher protection. I might well have triumphantly smirked at them. It's also quite possible that the counselor caught that smirk, because, after he dismissed them, he kept me on for an addendum to his lecture on the mountain ethos and the value of mutual loyalty. You're nothing but a little snitch, he told me in conclusion. But he was wrong. I was nothing but a wanton boy, Flycatcher was my name, and I was going to live forever.

2

The only girl who ever talked to me at the mountaineering lodge was Silvija. She was one of the oldest, and the best skier among them all. On the slopes, she was amazing; she went downhill at incredible speed, graceful like a comet. But when off the skis, she was an albatross, awkward, always sitting uncomfortably because she dealt with too much muscle in her thighs and hips—or so I remember, because, why else would she have talked to me? I was known as Flycatcher at the time. Yet she sat next to me, unforced, and she talked to me. I didn't know what to say, so, in trying to present some of the reasons why I turned out so blatantly weird— thereby bragging about it—I told her that I had once witnessed a suicide leap off the top of the building across the street and on the way down hit a horizontal antenna sticking out at someone's window, so that chunks of his brain stayed on the antenna grid. Why I made that up on the spot, to this day I do not know, but I did make it up: language and lies came to me as easily as stealing. I must've believed that having witnessed suicide would've given me access to knowledge not available to others, therefore impressive; what I saw and knew made me different from other boys; it made me belong to a different world, mature and deep. Death is not an event in life, but I imagined it within my life to make me appear cool and rub my skinny thighs with Silvija's. It occurred neither to me nor to Silvija at the time that the suicide's head would've snapped off the antenna rather than going through it as through a sieve and leaving brain remnants, like memories, on the hollow antenna ribs. It's also possible that she saw right through me, through the spectacle of my bullshit, might have recognized that Flycatcher was just a lonely wanton boy, so desperate for attention he was sacrificing suicides without compunction, making up gruesome details just to stay close to her and bask in the thick-thigh warmth of her downhill-skier body, hoping she might appreciate the narrative confidence, the arbitrary exactness of the detail, the poetic instinct, the brains. We sat in silence for a while, facing an ice-patched window against which a solitary, bedazzled fly kept bouncing. Why would he do something like that? was what she finally asked. I have no idea, I said. I cannot begin to imagine.

LOGICAL DISJUNCTION

Either the queen is dead or
     she crowns your hand

Either your fathers were kings or
     they died homeless paupers

Either your mother is a nigga nigga or
     she's a half-white nigga

Either race is a genetic experiment or
     it's a ransacked Section 8

Either humans use their claws or
     humans are consumed

Either history stutters or
     history was born mute

Either paradise is a congress of hoes or
     hell's rivers have no mouths

Either someone holds the mirror or
     someone else has no reflection

Either "they" means alla them there or
    "we" means alla us here

Either this is a free country or
    the dream is wildly overpriced

Either *hoard* is *fear* misspelled or
    lack's unlikely synonym

Either broke men leave nothing or
    nothing breaks death's weight

Either you wail ENOUGH into space and
    it is emptied breath inside an urn or
    it is hurricane to dust.

COGNOMINATE

after Nicole Homer

i name myself
> *rotting milk*
> *father's daughter*
> *clamshell, cracked against sand rock*
> *soap scum stuck in your hair after the lather rinses off*
> *son, or something like it*
> *teeth littered in grass, planted in soft earth*
> *sprout of my mother's stomach*
> *the potato you forgot at the back of the pantry until it started to grow again*
> *anything that isn't a word someone else tried to make me hold*

i keep cutting my lip open
as each new word finds a different way
to slice at my gums

eventually, every noise
just smells like iron

i wonder how many words i can fit
in my stomach before my belt breaks open
& the buttons go flying everywhere

you know the monty python sketch
where the man orders the left side of the menu
& the right side of the menu
& bursts only after eating a single mint
   (*it's only wafer thin*)

sometimes i feel like that
& i can't tell when the meal is ending
& i am getting to the mint

sometimes i say my own name
or some version of it
or a new thing i have just created
& it feels like splitting myself in half

i mean,
this is truly an exhausting thing

every morning i place a wafer under my tongue
prepared to swallow
at the first sign of trouble,
let it dissolve thin & sickly sweet

there are so many versions of me
sitting in so many people's throats
that now i am limescale
coating every pipe after the hard
water evaporates

there is actually very little difference
between who i was
& who i've called myself into
only less teeth now

THIS TRUTH ABOUT CHAOS

John Freeman

We are terrible people sometimes, writers.

If my father smelled of anything through my childhood, it was cut grass and sawdust. Most evenings, before dinner, I'd find him in the garage, standing in shirtsleeves before a table covered in screws and greasy rivets, wrestling with a machine. A lawn mower, a sprinkler head, some piece of pipe. If an appliance broke, he fixed it, and if it wasn't broken he made sure it would be by tinkering with it. My father wasn't particularly handy, but he grew up in a generation that distrusted objects they couldn't master. When these things resisted him he'd let loose a string of compound epithets and I knew it was time to lie low.

Even then, in my early teens, I understood his fiddling with tools was a displacement activity. By day my father ran a nonprofit family service agency that provided what the government no longer would. The agency employed social workers to counsel people going on or off welfare, drivers to deliver meals to shut-in seniors, patient and skilled therapists to operate a suicide hotline at its Sacramento offices. It was good work, and I know my father was proud of it, but I also

sensed—from being around him—that the job was like bailing a leaky boat. One day he arrived home flecked in blood: a client had cut her arms open and died in the office's entryway.

The state didn't fund these services and so part of my father's job involved scrounging five- and six-figure checks from the very people who'd voted to undo the government safety net that had once protected the poor and indigent. Occasionally, my two brothers and I were roped in to work the coat check at his fund-raisers. We'd put on our blue blazers with brass buttons and accept folded dollar bills to watch over the belongings of wealthy Californians who paid $250 for a dinner to benefit a good cause—a fraction of a fraction of what they'd probably received from trickle-down tax breaks. On one of these nights, I was amazed at how a few hours' worth of tips filled my pocket fatter than a month of delivering newspapers. Then I realized that was exactly what my father was probably thinking in that room, shaking hands, smiling with gritted teeth. His patrons' financial dandruff would keep his operation running.

This position of dependence made my father irate. It seemed obvious to him that if you had enough, you gave some away; if you had a lot, then the size of your giving should follow. But we were living through a time that has reached perhaps its apogee now, a period of defining poverty as a choice and mental-health problems as weakness and government intervention as a form of idiocy beyond words. One night in the middle of a heavy grant-writing period, my father nearly turned the dining table over with frustration. "What if I tell them *we help burned children*," he yelled at my mother, who, as usual, was trying to talk him down. "Do you think that'd be enough? We help *burned* children."

My father almost didn't become this person: the class warrior who rejected a silver spoon for a life of social work. Growing up he'd been a class clown and mama's boy who played football and drove a brand-new Chevy V8. His family lived in the Fabulous '40s, a Sacramento neighborhood made famous by the film *Lady Bird*. Governor Reagan was a neighbor; my grandfather, who'd been raised in San Francisco after the earthquake fire, was in the Gipper's cabinet. Meantime, my father drank and partied and very nearly didn't even get into community college. It was by the skin of his teeth that he'd later manage to transfer into Berkeley, where his father had paid his own way during the Depression, and after graduation my father was so lost he briefly worked as a prison guard before joining the seminary. Which he then dropped out of after reading Nietzsche. I don't know how he found

This position of dependence made my father irate.

social work, but he did and eventually, in his midthirties, realized it was what he was meant for.

As counselors, my parents both worked in a form of narrative therapy—people told stories to them to sort out who they were and why they were so troubled. Similarly, my parents told their own stories to us—in particular, my father's. Oddly, it was my mother imparting my father's origin story most often, not him. At nights, if he lost his temper, she'd slip into my room on tiptoes and explain how badly my father didn't want us to live the same way he had—zigzagging, emotionally neglected. That and work were why he was so tense.

I didn't for a second doubt her, nor do I now. I know my father loves us, I am lucky to have him in my life, and to believe this with all my heart. My father's approach to fathering, though, was to "flood the zone," to borrow a football phrase old *New York Times* editor Howell Raines used to describe his approach to covering big stories. No activity I participated in growing up went unchecked, unsupervised, or untested for nutritional value. If I appeared to have free time my father would dig up a reading list from a school district *back east*, as the East Coast was called. Or I'd be dispatched to earn a Boy Scout merit badge so rarely pursued it even stumped the

scoutmaster. *Huh, they have architecture?* By the age of thirteen, stoked by my father's horror stories of the career-less and dissolute—*You want to be driving a Subaru and watching Sacramento Kings games your whole life?!*—I'd interned in several possible careers—medicine, architecture, and even law—and found them wanting.

In essence, my father treated my brothers and me as if we were being homeschooled, even though we attended school for ten hours of the day. This was a luxury to have such care, but also a burden, because it is in the nature of adolescents to be fickle and lazy, to discard interests like snakeskin and find new things. We did all of this, and it incensed my father. He was so desperate for us to succeed as adults, he treated us like adults, explaining what could go wrong at adult levels—*Do you want to wind up in prison, maybe you start drinking and then what, you accidentally hit someone driving home at night?*—even giving us condoms at age ten. I socked mine away until they rotted; my older brother eventually used his; my little brother turned his into water balloons and threw them at passing cars.

My father had a weird and unexpected sense of humor in those days, but not about failure. Growing up in the shadow of his love, we felt like failures waiting to happen. This wasn't misinterpretation, because he often used those very words. Listening through the wall one night as

> My father had a weird and unexpected sense of humor in those days, but not about failure.

he tried to help my older brother complete his math homework, I heard my father shout over and over each time Andy offered up the incorrect answer: "Wrong! You're a failure! You're a failure! Just give up!" And then I heard my father storm out of the room, slamming the door, making the house shake.

The zoom and swerve of my father's anger was the weather system of those years and it was frankly terrifying. A conversation often escalated from questions across some unseen thermal to tornadic interrogation so fast it was bewildering. He wasn't a tall man, but he was *dense* and phenomenally strong, and we came to know this. My father once caught my older brother and me wrestling in our front yard and a split second after I saw his shoe in my peripheral vision we were airborne. He'd flung both of us into the bushes as if we were lightly packed duffel bags. It got worse and it was unpleasant and I spent a lot of my early teens in a constant state of fear.

My older brother bore the brunt of this fury; my younger brother assumed a posture of the victim; my response was to become very, very independent. I took on after-school activities and rarely turned up at home before seven. I became a reader, so my mind was literally elsewhere. Playing six sports a year, I sculpted my body into a defensive weapon. I didn't get into fights, but people would have to think twice before pushing me around. Including him. The result of these strategies was that I developed a sense of doubleness that has become permanent over time. As if I watch everything happen in front of me a moment before it actually happens, and then dispatch the person playing me to handle it.

For this reason, I have come to feel at home around volatile people. Around those who demand a lot and create the mood, who make decisions and set terms. It's familiar. I don't even need to deploy this doubleness; it just happens. Whenever I felt the ground shift, when I knew my father was at the edge's edge, I learned how to deflect and anticipate, I figured out when to disappear. I did this so well I became a seismologist of mood and could even predict the tremors before they happened. And so now, as a forty-four-year-old, when a fault line slips in virtually any situation, I am already halfway there to meet it. I have begun booting up a whole variety of de-escalation strategies—conversational, nonverbal, physical. In other words, without realizing it, my father spent a lot of my teenage years molding me perfectly into the shape of a receptive editor.

Someone who could adapt to a wide variety of intensities and insanities.

As I writer, I say this with affection and knowledge of my own insanities. We are terrible people sometimes, writers. Narcissistic, belligerent, single-minded, and strange. The rising forms of mania that accompany peculiarly small details are endless. I understand why. Writers are in control of their work and nothing else. And yet their survival often depends heavily on that *nothing else*. Getting reviews or teaching jobs or book sales over which they have often very little control. This is a recipe for intense anxiety. Even if you discount the attendant worries about whether work will last, if it is in fact any good, people also have to eat, they need health care (in America), they need roofs over their heads and school for their children, if they have them. Providing any significant part of this on a writer's salary is virtually impossible. It's ludicrous. We may not require the services my father's agency provided, but our needs are part of the same spectrum: domestic requirements cannot be ignored. They have to be taken care of and the money earned from writing almost never suffices. Even Zadie Smith and Jhumpa Lahiri teach, what does that tell you? Given the influence of reputations on grants and awards, the bind of dependency writers live under is ever more stressful.

I knew early on, watching my father work, and sitting next to my mother as she took down notes from patients dying of Parkinson's and AIDS, that I didn't have it in me to be on the front line of care for others. My mother spent most of my teenage years driving upward of 150 miles a day to remote houses to counsel people about to lose a loved one about what they were facing. It was grim and important and grinding work, and you needed more than belief to do it— you needed a temperament of patience and something else, something almost holy, I hesitate to say, to do it. I thought about this a lot when my mother too eventually fell ill, and then got worse, and finally became the kind of patient someone like her—a social worker in a car—came to visit. They were mostly there to talk to my dad, to see how he was doing, holding what must have felt like the earth on his shoulders all day. On the day she died, my father sent the social worker away. It was as if he knew right away that the next weight he would have to lift would be her absence. At first he'd want to do that alone.

I wished I had this temperament. I loved my mother dearly and admired her even more than my father for the way she contained all those terrible stories and made people feel better. When I became a writer, it didn't even occur to me to make a story up: she had been living proof it wasn't necessary. They were all around us, eating away at people's bodies. My father may have been the bully sometimes, but my mother was the one who taught me the hardest lesson. In hearing about just a few of her cases, it was clear to me that chaos was out there, waiting for all of us in some form or other. Usually lying in wait in our bodies. In the end, it would catch us. My father pressed down hard, sometimes too hard, thinking he'd protect us from this truth about chaos, and in so doing he made me into someone who would try to help those with a rage to shape it.

I made this connection not long ago. I was in Sacramento visiting my father. He lives there today with his second wife in the old neighborhood where he grew up, driving a car he would have made fun of back in my teenage years, and doing a lot of beautiful gardening, some volunteer work—like escorting women to clinics that provide abortions—and vigorous walking. One of the bewildering changes for me about his life since he remarried has been a shift in his domestic sphere. The home I grew up in was terrific but in a constant state of disarray. The house my father now lives in and its gardens could be a museum.

Pulling into it late one night on a visit, I was so confused as to doubt I'd reached the right address. Sitting there, engine idling, it brought me back to the late 1980s and early '90s, when no matter how hard I tried to avoid the house I lived in, I was beholden to it on the weekends.

Even when I had an away game or track meet, I had to spend thirty-six or more hours in our house. Living in the Central Valley meant you could plant, mow, prune, trim, and generally molest your yard for ten or eleven months out of the year. On weekends my father set to our lawns with a rage that was almost comical. One summer he ripped out the ivy in our palm tree one leaf at a time. Another summer he dug a sunken garden and planted eucalyptus trees so the pet rabbit we'd lost interest in had somewhere cool to graze. Almost every week she dug six feet down beneath the fence pilings and tunneled to freedom.

Every single task we performed in the yard was rapidly, hilariously undone by nature. Foxes ate grapes off the vine we planted. Raccoons nibbled the flower buds. The lawn browned in the baking sun just as fast as you watered it, and trying to get around sprinkler laws with slow-rotating backyard water dispersal units was dangerous. One Sunday morning I was woken by my father screaming in the kitchen—the thing had rolled over and nearly severed one of his gnarled ex-tight-end fingers.

I wish my mother were still here to fill me in on her version of this period of our lives together. She was the one who prised my father's forefinger from the jaws of death, and I think she also told him he had to stop hitting us. Because at some point in this time it ceased—and more and more often she'd shake me from a dream on a weekend morning, her face twisted in uncharacteristic anger, and yell at me to *go out there and help your father, he's fifty years old, he'll have a heart attack.*

So I'd lope out to the backyard and find my father with his back to the house. Tending the sunflowers or clipping weeds, laying down mulch for the rhododendrons. Sometimes he'd give me something to do, but as I got older, he'd send me away or I'd have to force him to let me help. I think he just wanted to be alone. Sometimes, we'd drive off to the nursery to buy fertilizer for the azaleas or some new flower he'd nestle in against one of the fences. By sundown he'd be sunburned and salt-streaked and very, very quiet. After dinner, as we watched the evening news or a basketball game, he'd ask my brothers and me for backrubs. He had a huge back, and it took all three of us. 🝐

Suji Kwock Kim

PRAYER FOR A SON

(Peace Hotel, Shanghai)

Gods of napalm, gods of cobalt and phosphorus,
gods of polybrominated diphenyl ether,
give us this day our daily lie:

of the war no one can talk about, or talk about not talking about,
of coup, counter-coup, and counter-countercoup,
of splinter groups and splinters of splinters.

The hooded bodies are roped down like dogs,
blindfolded and gagged, or heaving bile,
the lucky ones, because they're still alive.

I woke and slept and woke and slept
as if my disbelief could save him:
but no peace, no peace, in the Peace Hotel.

Lord of Morphine, Lord of Methamphetamine,
I am sick with a fever of never—
so airbrush away the corpses,

bring on the mail-order brides.
I woke and slept and woke and slept
but no peace, no peace, in the Peace Hotel.

PRAYER: AT THE MIGRANT HOSPITAL

Lord, I don't know
where you are, or if you are.

I pray every night
—but to what gods?—that he'll live.

Forgive me, faith,
for not feeling you:

I cannot not see
my son's closing eyes, so I don't believe

in belief, I believe in this wooden floor,
these cinder-block walls, the steel brace

soldering spine to skull, I believe
in every pock and crook of his bones,

every clotted hair on his blue-black scalp,
every lash, every nail, every pore, every breath—

Our Lady of Syringes, Our Lady of Pharmaceuticals,
Our Lady of Validol and Demerol and Haldol,

see him, spare him,
son I cannot save.

Yvonne Amey

BEHIND BARS, YOU SAID, THERE'S FREEDOM TO JOIN A CHAIN GANG

Let's leave the edge of whatever state we are in
for the City of Two Types of People:
the dead no one claims &
the others looking for faces.
Prince and his symbol are in heaven.
De Kooning and his mother are in heaven.
Jesus and daffodils make you happy.
For you, I grab this cross and bouquet from a funeral.
But there was always something about that still life
above Father's bed, its composition—him, smiling,
a boy, a Christmas tree,
a grief so deep a hundred bodies are buried in it.
See the blue like copper burning.
See how it rests under his skin.
See how the edge of the sun is him staring down at us forgetting.
Some of this is a lie and the first time I dreamed of him
I was running through a forest lathered
in acrylic and light and I was ripping off all my skin.

ADDICTS

And I remember how cold it was
and how the grayness in February followed
us to NA and group therapy
and I remember Jeremy
and how he couldn't keep his fingers out
of the narcotics box
how he confided *I don't think I can*
and I said *I don't think you can either*
and I remember late one night
he and I went out back
to bury what was missing in us
how a plume of ready rock
smoke kept us warm
and I remember there was ice
on the firs
and under our feet
and I remember how ill-fitting our skin felt
wrapped tightly around
bones we didn't know were dragging.

CLUTCH PERENNIALS

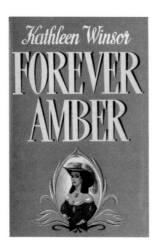

ON KATHLEEN WINSOR'S

Forever Amber

ALYSSA KNICKERBOCKER

When my mother was twelve, she found a book stuffed in the back of her mother's bookshelf. It was a thick, disintegrating paperback, held together by a rubber band. On the cover, a luscious woman with pinkish-blonde hair gazed seductively into the distance, her breasts heaving out of an extremely low-cut gown. It was very obviously not intended for a twelve-year-old. So she immediately took it up to her room and hid it.

There was not a lot of privacy available for surreptitiously reading steamy, highly inappropriate romance novels. This was the mid-1960s, the height of the baby boom, in the near suburbs of Detroit. Her father was a surveyor, and came home every evening dusty, in a dusty truck; her mother kept house, sewed clothes, cooked, did not drive. For the whole week after she found the book, she stayed up all night every night reading with a flashlight under the tent of her sheets until she passed out on the open page. She spent the week exhausted, constantly nervous that she'd be caught, and the book taken away before she finished it: an inconceivable tragedy.

Forever Amber, the story of a country girl who makes it big in seventeenth-century

England through her wits, ruthlessness, and beauty, was first published in 1944. Kathleen Windsor, the author, was an unknown, and the book was close to a thousand pages long – but it zoomed up the bestseller chart in the first week, and eventually sold millions of copies. People loved it and wildly disapproved of it in equal measure. It was banned in Massachusetts. The attorney general of that state asserted that the book was "obscene, indecent, and impure" and sifted through the text for evidence, finding "70 references to sexual intercourse; 39 to illegitimate pregnancies; 7 to abortions; 10 descriptions of women undressing . . . in the presence of men; 5 references to incest; 13 references ridiculing marriage; and 49 miscellaneous objectionable passages." There are, in fact, a lot more scenes with people undressing—but maybe the attorney general was only concerned with *women* undressing. I was frankly more piqued by the men.

I was about the same age as my mom had been when I read *Forever Amber*, but I didn't have to find it at the back of a bookshelf—my mother gave it to me. The crumbling paperback of her own youth was of course long gone, and it had been out of print for years, but she'd stumbled across a copy at a used bookstore. I was dubious. It was a doorstop of a book, an enormous historical novel. Luckily, you don't have to wait long for the action to begin.

We meet Amber St. Clare at age sixteen. She is Too Sexy for her little town. She has "tawny" hair and eyes and a natural, irrepressible sexuality: "There was about her a kind of warm luxuriance, something immediately suggestive to the men of pleasurable fulfillment—something for which she was not responsible but of which she was acutely conscious." All the other girls, obviously, hate her. A group of Cavaliers comes riding through, spreading the news that King Charles II is returning to England after years of exile, and so the novel kicks off with both the dawn of the English Restoration and a lusty spark between Amber and the hunkiest of the Cavaliers—a baron with the somewhat fratty name of Bruce Carlton—whose love she will chase fruitlessly for the rest of the book.

The rest of the book! How to sum it up? I'll try: After a hot rendezvous in the grass by a wishing well, Amber follows Bruce to London. Though he swears he will never marry her—and indeed, never does—she's in love, and besides, she has ambitions to be more than just a farm wife, making babies and sweeping floors. Bruce leaves her, pregnant, to go off to sea, as men do, so she marries a gross man with gross teeth who steals all her money and abandons her. She's dragged off to Newgate, the infamous debtors prison. Things look grim. But from here, she rises, grasping her way up and out of poverty, going from man to man like rungs on a ladder. From one man, money; from another man, a title. By the end of the book there's a pile of men behind her and she is a duchess, wealthy and gorgeous, mistress to the king of England, celebrated and envied and reviled. She has Made It. But she still doesn't have the one thing she wants: Bruce Carlton. He marries another woman, someone classier than she is, without her bombastic sexuality. Amber, after all, is still not "wife" material. And ironically, every step she's taken to try to get closer to him—to scale the class barriers and make herself into a person he could marry—has made her less so.

The plot is hilariously overpacked. Through Amber's sexual misadventures we experience the British Civil Wars and the execution of Charles I, the Restoration, the Great Fire of London, the Black Plague, the settlement of America, not to mention Amber's four husbands, many lovers, and a handful of murders. But the beating heart of the book is the on-off relationship between Amber and Bruce. It is frankly sexual, unabashedly physical. None of the other books I'd ever read talked about romance this way, as though physical attraction was to be found at the root of it. Romance had thus far been cerebral, intellectual—Anne and Gilbert, a meeting of the minds. This book had a fierce, animalistic tone to it that mesmerized me. At twelve, I knew the basics of sex but what I didn't quite grasp was why anyone would *want* to do it. *Forever Amber* answered this question, resoundingly.

I recently came upon *Forever Amber* in my local library. After its early success, it seems to have faded away, dated and a little soapy, not meant to endure as great literature of the era. But it was reissued in 2002, and a curling paperback, obviously much-read, sat on the shelf. I planned to skim through, reread a couple of clutch scenes—my favorite was always the part where Bruce and Amber both contract the Black Plague and nurse each other through, buboes and all—but I glanced at the first page and was doomed.

I read the whole thing in a week, staying up late at night, exhausted all day. Some of the more cliché romance novel tropes stood out this time around—many of the peripheral characters are either villains or angels; they are described as having "flashing purple eyes" and bite their fists in moments of high emotion. But Winsor had real writing chops, and a deep understanding of the era borne of the hundreds (!) of books she read while completing the novel. The passages depicting seventeenth-century London are beautifully done. She describes the hundreds of ringing church steeples rising through the crowded city, and then in the next sentence, the sewage, the burning fires, the poverty. Noblewomen sweep through with black velvet opera masks, their dresses stained in the armpits, their hems caked in mud. You can smell everything.

Another surprise: the novel is slyly, strangely feminist. I wanted to stand up and cheer for Amber's confident sexual agency, her refusal to be ashamed, her frank enjoyment of sex. The book is matter-of-fact about abortion and the devastating consequences for women who are forced to carry unwanted pregnancies. And through it all there is the sharply made point that women have fewer avenues to success available to them than men do. Amber is often offered but one way forward, then harshly judged for taking it.

Forever Amber is not a perfect book or a great work of literature—it's a bit of a hot mess, a mash-up of romance-genre tropes and historical texture, with some skillful craftsmanship underneath, carrying everything forward. But I didn't care, reading along, if this plot point or that one was plausible or not; swept up by Amber, I just cared how she navigated it. I read every page as though I'd never read it before. As a writer in the throes of trying to finish her own book, I found it helpful to be reminded that there's something to be said for a ripping good read.

My grandmother died when I was sixteen. In my memories from childhood, she is always in the kitchen, in her housedress with her hair pin-curled, a soft dark mass that turned white over the years. There was a small black-and-white television on the kitchen table that was always turned to a soap opera: *As the World Turns* or *Days of Our Lives*. She kept them on all day, smoking her long cigarettes by the window, sipping from a strong manhattan. She was sweet, and gentle, and sometimes seemed a little sad. I knew that one of her children, a girl, had died very young, of appendicitis, before my mother was born, but she didn't like it when we asked questions, or tried to jimmy the lock on the wooden trunk upstairs that held just a few things that had belonged to four-year-old Gretchen—a tiny pair of leather shoes, a faded doll. She loved small pleasures: chocolate Jordan almonds, having someone lightly scratch the insides of her elbows.

Once my mother had secretly read all thousand of the pages, she marched triumphantly downstairs to confess. My grandmother would be appalled, but what could she do about it now? My mother swept into the kitchen. "I read *Forever Amber*," she announced defiantly.

"Oh!" my grandmother said, and then, with a dreamy look on her face, gave a long sigh. "Wasn't it *wonderful*?"

ON DR. RUTH BARNETT AND
DOUG BAKER'S

They Weep on My Doorstep

TANA WOJCZUK

"The first abortion of which I ever had any experience was my own," writes Dr. Ruth Barnett in her 1969 memoir, *They Weep on My Doorstep*. The book is as gutting as the title suggests. For more than forty years, Barnett ran an illegal but aboveground abortion clinic in Portland, Oregon, and in that time nearly forty thousand women came to her for abortions. Abortion was legal under common law in the United States until 1880, but newspapers of the nineteenth century frequently reported on women who had died from the procedure—not because abortions were particularly dangerous, but because there weren't enough trained doctors willing to provide them. During Barnett's lifetime, women seeking illegal abortions frequently died

from a perforated uterus, infection, and septic shock. "Many Women Pay Death Penalty after Abortions" was the headline of a 1966 *Washington Post* article that included gruesome descriptions of girls giving themselves abortions on their beds with a mirror and a sharp object, or injecting soap or inserting medications into their vaginas. "Girls go through hell," warned one Catholic doctor in the article, "abortion is a painful, terrible procedure." But Barnett argues that, when performed by a well-trained doctor, abortions can be safe and relatively painless. "I never lost a patient," she writes. Barnett was seventy-five and dying of cancer when she told her story to *Oregon Journal* staff writer Doug Baker. Barnett, who wore a different colored wig every time she met her amanuensis, was waiting for a judge to decide whether she would be sent to prison for performing abortions.

They Weep on My Doorstep begins in 1911 with Barnett's unexpected pregnancy at sixteen. The father was twenty and when she told him, he denied responsibility. Barnett had recently started a new job as an assistant in a dentist's office. She one day got to talking with a patient whose style and confidence she had always admired. Barnett was both shocked and excited to find out that the woman was a prostitute. Hesitantly, Barnett asked what she would do if she became pregnant. The prostitute soon guessed Barnett's problem and led her to an abortionist named Dr. Watts. Barnett was familiar with the horror stories: girls drinking lye or pretending to "go insane" to get doctors to agree to give them abortions. But she soon discovered that Watts was ready to help her, and that his clinic was clean and professional looking. The relief was overwhelming. Barnett's abortion had "everything to do" with her becoming an abortion doctor, she writes, because it was performed not in a back alley but "smoothly and painlessly" in Watts's office.

During World War I, Barnett writes, the need for abortion spiked: more hasty sex before men went to war, more "Dear Jane" letters to pregnant, desperate girls back home, and more women than ever coming to abortion clinics to beg for help. After the war, Barnett went to work with her friend Alys Bixby Griff at her clinic as an assistant and then in 1929 went to work with Dr. Watts. It was Dr. Watts who encouraged her to go back to school to train as a naturopath and by the mid 1930s she had her own practice. At the time, doctors like Barnett, Watts, and Griff operated in a gray market, where abortions, though illegal, were tolerated. But this meant that doctors were not protected, and an election year, a change in government, could make them criminals. Watts would later die in prison, a convicted abortionist, and Barnett would be sent to prison several times. Each time she reemerged and began practicing again.

During World War II, demand for abortion again put a strain on the few clinics that offered that service (and those who did offer it soon found themselves doing nothing else). Barnett never turned away a woman who couldn't pay, but this sometimes meant that she became a bill collector on her patients' behalf. She tells the story of a pregnant girl whose boyfriend was the son of a wealthy man who was a powerful public figure. Sitting with her patient, Barnett saw that the girl's hands were stained deep red. The girl was poor, and to raise money for her abortion she, her mother, and her siblings had taken jobs picking berries. Barnett called the girl's boyfriend and his mother into her office. She noticed that the mother's nails were the same deep red color as the girl's berry-stained hands. The boy refused any responsibility for the pregnancy and it was only when Barnett threatened to call his father that he convinced his mother to pay for the abortion in full.

They Weep on My Doorstep is a dizzying book, and an oddly brilliant one. Chapters alternate between Barnett's story, larger cultural and political movements during this tipping point for women's reproductive rights, and the individual stories of women (including Barnett) chosen as a counterargument or reproof against anti-abortion rhetoric. The aperture of the book keeps changing, preventing the reader from sinking into complacency. *They Weep on My Doorstep* is by turns hopeful and devastating, and reveals the cruelty of a system that makes women beg for their lives. It combats that cruelty with medical matter-of-factness. At times this straightforwardness can seem steely, as when Barnett tells an eleven-year-old rape victim to try to forget about what happened to her. The story is uneven, rough-edged, told by a dying woman. *They Weep on My Doorstep* is a message in a bottle.

On February 5, 1968 Barnett entered the Oregon Women's Penitentiary. During the five and a half months she served (out of a two-year sentence) she watched on television the assassinations of Martin Luther King, Jr. and RFK; her grandson was injured in Vietnam. At the end of the book, she writes that, "at 75, I cannot hope to see universal law reform." She would die of cancer four years before Roe v. Wade.

If prostitution is the world's oldest profession, abortion is a close second. Wherever there are human actors there is human error. This is as true for designing fail-safes on a nuclear reactor as it is for having sex. Or as Einstein put it, "There are two things that are infinite, the universe and human error." If we accept that abortion is inevitable, who is served by criminalizing it? The bottle washes up with Barnett's reply inside: when the doctors who serve women operate in a gray area of the law they are vulnerable. Laws that ensure abortions are safe and simple to obtain don't make abortion more common; it makes the law more humane.

Wealthy women will always be able to get an abortion, argued Supreme Court Justice Ruth Bader Ginsburg, who believed Roe should have rested on equal protections rather than a right to privacy. But in many parts of America, poor and working-class women still can't find a doctor trained and willing to give them a safe abortion. In a recent Supreme Court case about reproductive rights in Texas, Justice Ginsburg noted how many women lived over 100 miles from the nearest clinic. The response was that they could always go to New Mexico.

When I lived in Portland, I passed the downtown office building where Barnett had her clinic every day on my way to a job bussing tables. I had no idea how many women had gone through those doors in tears and emerged breathing freely. This shared history is largely invisible. *They Weep on My Doorstep* is not just a memoir; it is a vision we can aspire to, that when the women we love need abortions, and they will need them, they will be met with the skill and compassion Barnett showed her patients.

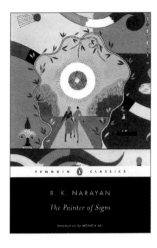

ON R.K. NARAYAN'S

The Painter of Signs

BY KAVITA DAS

For two decades, a volume of Indian writer R. K. Narayan's short stories (*The Grandmother's Tale and Selected Stories*, 1994) and well-known novel (*The Guide*, 1958) have sat on my bookshelves, moving with me from home to home, but remaining otherwise untouched. As an Indian American—and in the last five years, an Indian American writer—I've felt a nagging obligation to read and have an opinion on books by Indian writers, past and present. Yet my excitement over new books by current writers across the diaspora, combined with the reality of being a slow reader, has meant that I've felt compelled to keep Narayan's books in my orbit, but less inclined to actually read them. I haven't even read the works of the late Indian poet and writer who shares the same full name as my mother (Kamala Das).

Then, about a year ago, while rummaging through my neighborhood secondhand bookstore, I came across *The Painter of Signs*, a Narayan novel of which I hadn't heard. He was a prolific writer, publishing more than a dozen novels, numerous short stories, and myriad other work over several decades starting in the mid-1930s, before passing away in 2001. *The Painter of Signs*, published in 1976, struck me as bold for its time, yet its premise is particularly relevant to ours: the clash of gender norms couched within the broader clash of progress against tradition. Like several of his other works, it takes place in Malgudi, Narayan's fictional evocation of small-town South India. But unlike most of them, this novel explores not just love but sex, and gender politics, especially women's roles and reproductive health.

In the wake of the #MeToo movement, countries East and West have been forced to reexamine how sexual impropriety and sexual violence impact gender equity. Around the same time as Brett Kavanaugh's Supreme Court confirmation process, the Indian Supreme Court struck down Section 377 of the Indian Penal Code, which, in essence, had criminalized gay sex. The decision marked progress and was cause for celebration—celebration nonetheless set into relief by the country's troubling record of sexual violence against women and girls. A 2018 global survey cited this as the reason for ranking India as the most dangerous country for women. With these events in these two countries as both backdrop and catalyst, I embarked on reading *The Painter of Signs*.

Raman, the thirtysomething eponymous character, revels in his life of words, both those he selects and paints onto his signs and those he pores over in the old, worm-eaten books he picks up from the local bookstall. He fancies himself "a lettering artist," and longs for a life where his signs matter, where the care he takes in crafting signs that reflect his penchant for finding the precise words and rendering them in the perfect hue and font, is valued. Instead, as a small-town sign maker, he attempts to hustle and haggle, but quickly capitulates to the demands of his customers on matters of style and price.

Then a young woman named Daisy arrives in Malgudi, with her zealous, unthwartable mission to curb the area's population through family planning measures, thereby improving the lives of girls and women and reducing poverty. Daisy is unlike the women of Malgudi, eschewing cultural norms of what a single woman can say and do. As a person of action, Daisy recruits the soon-besotted Raman into her public awareness campaign, pulling him along to surrounding villages to paint signs that promote the virtues of family planning: "With just one, we will be happier." But Raman, who finally has the opportunity to put his sign-making skills in service of an important cause, is more interested in satisfying Daisy, and rather ambivalent about her mission.

Raman prides himself on being a man of reason and truth, yet he is confounded by Daisy's frankness when it comes to sex, a contrast to his carefully circumscribed conversations with male acquaintances. I was pleased that this forty-two-year-old Indian book explores gender norms and sex, but I was shocked when one night, Raman attempts to seduce, and if necessary force himself on, Daisy, foiled largely because Daisy absconds into a tree. In the aftermath, Raman wavers between shock, guilt, and defiance, using chauvinism cloaked as "reason" to justify his actions—actions that could've resulted in rape. Though Daisy is deeply disappointed in Raman, she's made even more upset by his inability to take responsibility and show remorse. These scenes eerily reminded me of the irate reactions some men, including Kavanaugh, exhibit when confronted with allegations made against them, and when asked to explain their improper behavior.

It's no surprise that Raman and Daisy's relationship is doomed, but what is surprising is that this alarming incident, which occurs about halfway into the novel, is not what ends it. Although I was initially rankled by this episode, upon further contemplation I wonder if it speaks to the complexity of sexual misconduct and the dilemmas regarding what happens to offenders and the possibility of redemption. What if we are just halfway into our collective narrative on these issues?

Narayan's rendering of Raman and Daisy seems at once reflective of the cultural norms of his time while also nodding toward the need for progress. While he imbues Raman and Daisy with both admirable qualities and flaws, they struggle with how to relate to the opposite sex in a country and era straddling tradition and modernity. Ultimately, because of Narayan's deftness in portraying these compelling characters, readers perceive them through their own lenses: some will see Daisy as a bold heroine who transcends gender expectations of domesticity while helping other women; others will empathize with Raman's struggle to adapt to changing gender norms.

I was born in the US to a South Indian mother who is an obstetrician gynecologist, but I grew up in a household that didn't talk about sex or sexuality. I learned about "the birds and the bees" thanks to the New York City public school system and whispered conversations on the playground. Both the book and my experiences underscore the power and persistence of cultural mores. The Painter of Signs takes place in 1972, two years before I was born, on a faraway continent, yet I see myself in its characters. Like Daisy, I'm an idealist who went to work, spending fifteen years of my life trying to make the world a better place by tackling housing inequities, public health disparities, and racial injustice. But I also relate to Raman's passion for words and books, and his appreciation of good food and a proper cup of coffee.

The tension between Raman's and Daisy's differences first attracts them to each other, then tears them apart, and, I now realize, that tension has existed in me, often erupting as I grappled with finding my place in the world. Are my words better used in service of literature—writing for writing's sake—or as propaganda for a crucial cause? When harnessed, this tension fuels my work. It catalyzed my ambition to rebrand a thirty-year-old racial justice organization with a name befitting its crucial mission, and it sparked my desire to write the life story of an overlooked woman-of-color artist. I hope it continues to galvanize and complicate my writing, irrespective of what my writing is in service to, just as I hope to plumb more works by Narayan, mirrors for examining the thorny complexities of our world and for considering my place in it.

ON AMA ATA AIDOO'S

Our Sister Killjoy, or Reflections from A Black Eyed Squint

BY THIRII MYO KYAW MYINT

I read Ama Ata Aidoo's *Our Sister Killjoy* for the first time in November of 2009. I was grappling with an intense and enduring sense of disorientation following my return to Brown University after a summer teaching at a charity school and orphanage in Myanmar. I was born in Burma in 1989—days before the country's name was changed and a year after the second military coup—but my family left in 1990, when I was a baby, and returned only once, in 1995, when I was too young to remember the visit. The summer I spent in Myanmar thus constituted my first experience of the country, as well as my first encounter with the "least-developed" world, formerly known as the "third world," a world still reeling from the ongoing effects of European colonization. I had expected to experience culture shock when I arrived in Yangon, but instead it was when I returned to Providence that I felt deeply estranged from American consumerist culture, our culture of waste and exploitation. I was repulsed by the privilege that surrounded me, and at the same time recognized it as my own. My trip to Myanmar, for example, was funded by the Jack Ringer Summer in Southeast Asia Fellowship, an award made possible by Ringer, a Brown alum from Evanston, Illinois, who had served in Burma in 1952. "Served" is the verb used in the grant description to explain what Ringer did in Burma. To serve, to provide service: whether as a member of the military, as a missionary, or as a volunteer I do not know. The language of the grant seems to suggests that it does not matter.

Like me, the protagonist of *Our Sister Killjoy*—a young Ghanaian woman nicknamed Sissie—is a student from a postcolonial country who is awarded a grant to travel abroad. Like me, she is made aware of the shocking extent of global inequalities through her travels. Over the course of the book, Sissie struggles to emotionally process what she learns, and to "operate meaningfully" despite or through her disillusionment. First published in 1977, two decades after Ghana achieved independence from the British, *Our Sister Killjoy* is a genre-defying book that is divided into four sections: "Into a Bad Dream," "The

Plums," "From Our Sister Killjoy," and "A Love Letter." I hesitate to call these sections chapters because, though they are arranged chronologically, they are narratively and formally disjointed. Within the sections themselves, Aidoo's sentences are unstable—blocks of prose give way to centered stanzas, ellipses often take the place of periods, and sometimes an entire page will hold just a single word or a fragment.

Though *Our Sister Killjoy* has been called "experimental" I resist using that word, with its connotations of play and amateurism, to describe what Aidoo does in her book. To me, it seems that Aidoo is not *experimenting* with a language that is already given, already at her disposal, but instead *creating* a language that she can use. In the last section of the book, "A Love Letter," which is epistolary in form, as the title suggests, Sissie begins her letter, "My Precious Something, First of all, there is this language. This language." This language is the one in which I am also writing. English, a colonial language for both Aidoo and me, a language that was violently forced upon our ancestors. Later in her letter, Sissie asks, "What positive is there to be, when I cannot give voice to my soul and still have her heard? Since so far, I have only been able to use a language that enslaved me, and therefore, the messengers of my mind always come shackled?" How does one write a love letter in such a language? How does one write a book?

Our Sister Killjoy, I think, is Aidoo's answer to this question. It is a book whose language is sensitive and agile enough to explore the complexities and contradictions of postcolonial and diasporic subjecthood. Aidoo's third-person narrator is at times gentle, bitter, sarcastic, funny, and unpredictable, but rarely pedantic or plaintive. As a protagonist, Sissie is neither romanticized nor victimized by the narrator, nor is she allowed to romanticize or victimize herself. In the aforementioned passage from "A Love Letter," for example, Sissie answers her own rhetorical question about using "a language that enslaved" her with self-deprecating humor. She writes, "I know you would scream at me, full of laughter [. . .] 'Shackled? Sissie, your thoughts? Don't you think you are overdoing the modesty bit?'" In another section, when Sissie is confronted with the poverty of the Africans and West Indians she meets in England, the narrator tells us, Sissie "became sad. So sad she wanted to cry." In the very next paragraph, however, the narrator says, "that period lasted only a short time. Very soon, she started getting angry. Then she became very angry." The narrator does not elevate either Sissie's sadness or her anger, however, and instead dismisses both emotions as markers of her immaturity: "Our poor sister. So fresh. So touchingly naive then."

In a way, *Our Sister Killjoy* can be read as a bildungsroman in which the protagonist receives an education in global inequality and injustice. For example, in the beginning of "Into a Bad Dream," Sissie suspects that

her journey [to Germany] must
have had something to do with
people's efforts
 'to make good again;'

but it isn't until the third section, "Our Sister Killjoy," that the narrator asserts that scholarship students like Sissie were the recipients of the leftovers of imperial handouts:

> Post-graduate awards.
> Graduate awards.
> It doesn't matter
> What you call it.
>
> But did I hear you say
> Awards?
> Awards?
> Awards?
>
> What
> Dainty name to describe
> This
> Most merciless
> Most formalised
>
> Open,
> Thorough,
> Spy system of all time:
>
> For a few pennies now and a
> Doctoral degree later,
> Tell us about

> Your people
> Your history
> Your mind.
> Your mind.
> Your mind.

As a young student who already knew that I would have to rely on more awards, grants, scholarships, and benefactors such as Jack Ringer to continue my education, I read *Our Sister Killjoy* as both a cautionary tale and an exemplary one. On the one hand, passages like the one I quoted above spoke to and affirmed the fear I had always had of being tokenized; Aidoo made me feel less alone in that fear, but I also understood that if my fear was valid it was because the threat of neocolonialism was also valid, and I had to protect myself. On the other hand, *Our Sister Killjoy* was maybe the most honest, vulnerable, and risk-taking book I had read, and it showed me one example of how to be critical of institutions and systems without being dogmatic, how to be a "killjoy" without losing my sense of humor. At a time in my life when I felt utterly incapable of making sense, much less art, out of what I had witnessed of systemic inequality and injustice, *Our Sister Killjoy* gave me a language that I could use to process my experience. It showed me that it was possible to write in any language that was available, even this one. 🝮

Gabriel Fried

THE TRUTH

I take you out beyond the fence
to where the dead dog dug a hole.
It's not yet dark or cold.
I say I've told our parents.

Above the branches phone wires
give off an ancient hum.
Remember the noise last summer?
The cicadas were a bonfire

of sound we caught and dared
each other to eat alive.
I couldn't chew one when I tried.
It moved in my mouth like prayer,

then when I opened it was gone—
vanished like sacrifice.
You said that I was lying,
that I spit it out or hid it with my tongue.

But a lie is something you can prove,
the blooming side of a dying tree.
We're here, I say from part of me.
You think I speak to you.

GATHERING SWALLOWS

The first time we met you quoted "To Autumn,"
And gathering swallows twitter in the skies,
when I said poems can't just be images—
a glimpse, you said, superseding rhetoric,
your back so straight you sat a head taller
than anybody else at that dinner,
so I could see you thinking as you spoke.
Though now I wonder, if he wasn't dying,
could even Keats have pulled off that ending?
Our second winter, you pull strands of hair
across a novel's page, I tinsmith poems.
For a while it was enough just to clasp each other.
How long will it last to build a house together?
Raise a child? What's the *argument*?

REVISION

We don't create the world we envision.
We don't become the change we'd like to see.
The writing that turned out the way I'd planned
wasn't poetry. The loves I couldn't stand
to lose were just the ones who had to go.
If God exists, we've disappointed him
not through our failings, but by definition.
Take some comfort in that, Christian.
Take some comfort in this work you've done.
It's all the truth your back could bear.
Mankind is built to alter, not accept.
Why else would we tear down the woods' cathedral
everywhere, which is the world we'd choose
but can't, because it is already there?

THE GREAT LAKES

My wife, the one I thought I'd never have—
because does any of us believe we deserve
to be happy in this life?—lets my daughter paint
her toenails a sloppy silver as my aunt smokes
a second cigarette and pages through photos
on her phone so I can see how the car looked
after my cousin wrecked it last month
in a past-midnight field near the poultry
processing plant just a half mile from Grandma's
unsold house—high on meth or heroin
or maybe not high at all but fighting
her hunger—while I pick through this dead
girl's jewelry just as starved for something
to hold on to as those feckless gulls pecking

the sand a few feet away. The sun is shining
brighter than the gold-plated necklace
I fasten around my neck and swear to wear
forever, and even though scientists are finding
nicotine in the water and oxy in the mussels,
my cousin's kids are down there at the edge
of the beach screaming their heads off
with the pure joy of plunging below the surface.
It's not hard to feel good watching the waves.
But my aunt needs me to believe in the glass
and the blood, and her daughter's body
a thing unidentifiable, a thing none of us
had really seen in years. She needs me to understand
that her pain is water as far as the eye can see.

FICTION

Raw Season

Xavier
Navarro Aquino

I. SHADOW DANCING

The Dominican cats call it fukú but we call it fufú. An incantation said to be a curse. A medley brewed with a nip of postcolonial flavor, left behind in the Caribbean. Inherited through the dead and the living, even family members get in on the spell-slinging. Some say in order for a fufú to work, it needs a vessel. Something beyond the uttered words, a familial scar, or a melody as dark as a tormented bolero performed by a strung-out salsero.

Ma once told me that she cast a fufú on Pa, in case he ever got any funny ideas. All those sheets and good-fortuned shirts Ma anointed with her brujería, and Pa so proudly wore, carried the stains of fufú. This was when my parents preached maintenance of family traditions. Before Yamil grew old enough to keep a memory. Most fools didn't buy into our old master spells, talk of slaves and overseers be damned. We boricuas chalked it up to old curses and legacies. Yet Ma was convinced she could hold on to all of us with her fufú after Tío Raul croaked. Pa, Yamil, me.

El cementerio municipal of Lares was where all of Ma's family was buried. The gravesites were cement plots, heated past boiling point when the sun showed up, slippery when wet. Tío Raul's funeral was set for a Saturday. It was summer and humid. The Sahara dust felt like tear gas used to suffocate and drown lungs. I fussed when Ma commanded us to get ready for Raul's funeral. I was busy roleplaying in our yard. *Star Wars* mania had finally graced our small town and all I wanted to be was the scoundrel, Han, off on one of his schemes.

Ma wore a white Sunday dress and a pink-laced summer hat, her small face hidden behind large round sunglasses. She looked as though she was headed to a Communion, something uplifting. The contrast of the dress against her skin gave her a radiance that haloed around her. Even the changos stopped their scavenging to catch a glimpse. It all masked a frustration. An anger that moved the gravel she walked on. Something about Raul's funeral arrangements had set her off and we were going to the velorio with ulterior motives.

Pa contradicted her look. His curly Afro and lighter skin made Ma stick out more. Even though he was dressed sharp as a knife, next to Ma, he brought down her cachet. So she stomped a good two feet away from him. I'd decided to sport the expected black-on-black tie and shirt. Black casual from top to bottom made it unnoticeable when the sun decided to shoot strong heat our way.

Our dying Corolla backfired its way up the steeping hillside and we parked slanted, among the cars barely able to maintain their friction with the road. Yamil didn't make the trip. Ma said he was too young and was safer at home in Santana, in case we got caught in a stray deluge. Ma never enjoyed driving through Lares because of the rain.

In Lares, there was a known fear that shit could get real slushy in a storm—the ground would easily sink beneath you if it rained for more than two days. Village soothsayers (aka town drunks) never grew tired of the Hurricane San Felipe II prophecies. Said it was bound to happen to Lares any day. God's retribution for fighting against our master. Contrition for El Grito a little over a century ago. And the people of Lares would welcome it with open arms. "Let us sink right into the ocean, better to float dead and free than to serve a life in chains." That was Raul's song and dance. No surprise how happy his friends were to bring him all the way home when he died. These were all the talks. How important he was to the public because he was an artist. How he needed to become a spectacle for all to see as if his body became one of his paintings set up to auction. Those same friends chanted with conviction, "Get him out and away from San Juan, from that Muñoz Maríne–loving city. La ciudad del traidor."

We walked into the boxed building where they held Raul. A narrow corridor led us to the room he was in. Outside the door, Tío's picture was atop a gold painted podium next to a notebook registry and a black pen. And next to his portrait stood a trifold picture frame with photos of him dancing. One different in each frame. But in every one of them, he waltzed with a toddler. I couldn't help but feel cold. He was smiling there, his hips contorted beautifully. The child clutched against his ankle in fear.

"That's you, Paqo," Pa said. "A year after you were born."

> The Dominican cats call it fukú but we call it fufú. An incantation said to be a curse.

How close we seemed there, frozen in motion. I must've held on to him tightly, as if the music playing in that room was urgent. If it ended, I would fall to my clumsy knees and be left abandoned.

"Why do we have to sign our name in, Pa? Tío's not keeping count." Pa looked down at me through his sunglasses. He grabbed me by the shoulder and took me aside. He didn't say a word. Just knelt down and pointed his finger at me. Ma made her way through the door after signing her name. Pa shoved me into the room as he signed his name and mine. There were velvet curtains lining all four walls. At the front of the room sat an open coffin and a white veil covering the wooden casket.

I noticed my cousins and Tía Carmen—Ma's sister—speaking to each other next to the coffin. Her tight dress was hugging her love handles, her square face caked with makeup. I walked over and kissed her cheek. Then I saw him: Raul. He was clasping a crucifix and his skin was a dark green rust color, his smile forced into place. The AC vents were directly overhead and it was cold. Ma was standing over Tío with her sunglasses still on.

> "If you want to act tough, we can play that game outside. Go and pay your respects, mijo."

"Say hello, Paqo," Tía Carmen said. She swept me forward. I looked around and wanted to disappear. Ma turned to Tía Carmen and said something softly, her hands pointing at Tío, then outside.

I snuck behind Ma and hurried to the seats in the back. Pa entered the room and let out a sharp whistle.

"Family sits in the front, mijo," he said.

"I don't want to sit there. It's cold."

"Move it. Don't make me drag you."

He pinched my thigh but I didn't budge. My eyes watered. He moved close to my ear.

"If you want to act tough, we can play that game outside. Go and pay your respects, mijo," he whispered. I shook my head. "I'm not going to ask you again, Paqo."

All of those strange people near me tried giving me sympathy grins. Pa placed his hands on my shoulders and escorted me next to Ma. She didn't move once. Stayed speaking incantations to herself.

I didn't know Tío much. The stories told of him were said in snippets, incomplete songs on a transistor radio. His eyes were painted on. His long lashes resembled the strokes of a pincel detailing a woman's exaggerated stare. Some of his paintings were framed and hanging on a panel next to the wooden casket.

Ma jolted out of her trance and petted my hair before moving next to Tía. I wanted to leave but Pa sunk his talons into me and forced me next to Ma. He leaned into the plastic face of Raul and said a few words under his breath before walking to the entrance. He stood there and looked over everyone. I glanced at him to see if I could make a sly escape like he had but he quickly lifted his finger.

Tía Carmen was difficult to talk to, she would listen to you if you spoke, but it was superficial. She'd play along, banging her head in absent approval and let out forced grins until her boredom reached its tipping point. She'd interrupt you just to start her rants.

"Monsy, I spoke with Pedro. The undertaker. As soon as we arrived. He wanted to know if we were going to pay for the service with the installment plan."

Ma tried to brush off her comment but Tía poked at her shoulder.

"Monsy? I don't know about you but . . ."

"Ya, Carmen!" Ma snapped back. "You know why I'm here. This is not how we do things. This is not what Raul wanted. I'm here to clean up your mess."

"What mess? To think, you had it easier . . ."

"Cállate, Carmen!"

The people around us stopped talking.

"I'm not paying for any of this. This ceremony. Tú sabes como se hace esto. En familia! En casa!"

"Now you're all into traditions and customs. Qué bonita, Monsy. La más tradicional."

Ma tromped her way to the door.

"Not here, Carmen!"

"And where are you going to put him? Hmm? Does Paquito know about your beautiful Raul?"

The way she said it made Ma stop in her tracks. Tía had something up her sleeve. Something on Ma, or Pa, or Raul. Maybe it was all that fufú. Fufú misfiring? Ma's spellbinding falling out of tune?

"I'm leaving soon, you know. Laly and me want to go to La Brava and play la Loto. See if tonight is the night," Tía said. Another one of her power moves. She pampered her hair and winked at me.

"Go ahead. We'll do the velorio in the trunk of our car if we have to," Ma said. She pressed her hand to the door and on her way out said her final piece. "Don't ever throw that in my face again. Never use Raul against me."

Tía eyed Ma as she left the velorio. Pa quickly shadowed her out of the room.

Tía then sat on a chair and tugged me to the seat next to hers.

"Wonder what's up her chocha? Let me tell you something, Paqo." I shuffled in place because I didn't want to be there next to her. Tía Carmen—the type that didn't give two fucks what occasion she found herself in. You could always depend on her to spew her thoughts without a strainer.

"Raul was as good of a man as he could be, Dios lo bendiga. He really was. But you don't get very far with all that he got himself involved with. And I'll tell you something else. Your madre better set you straight. That locura runs en tu sangre."

"No. No it doesn't."

"Yes, Paqo! Yes it does. That locura can make anyone go crazy. Look at him. He lost so much weight. Started talking all tecato and sleeping around with many women. Those putas got him hooked on perico. After that, all he did was scratch himself raw. His skin became as coarse as a nail file. It's your family curse, Paqo. Look at what it does. He lost hair too. You see him now?"

She pointed at the casket in front of us. I glanced over, trying not to make eye contact with Tía.

"That is not his hair," she said. "He looks like a freaking payaso. Qué barbaridad."

The threads on his head were glossy and silver. Against his dark skin the wig glowed in the same way Ma's white dress glowed. Raul was peaceful now. With a full head of hair. For some reason, I started to tremble.

"Looks stupid, doesn't it?" Tía whispered into my ear.

"He looks handsome," I said defiantly.

"Well. That's not the word I would use, but that's cute you think so."

There was a long uncomfortable silence. We both stared absently at Tío. He could hear us there talking. Pa never talked about the dead. And when everyone seemed to embrace stories and exchange any good tales about the deceased, Pa was the first to leave. Said nothing good comes from dwelling on people that can no longer breathe.

I tuned in to some of the surrounding tales about Raul. His mystical side steps. His merengue rhythm whenever he fell hard for the sway of a lady. How he painted to boleros. Especially to his famous cousin Felipe "La Voz" Rodriguez, who reigned supreme on the airways and in live shows with his smash hit bolero, "La Última Copa."

"You know, Paqo, he killed her," she finally said, jolting me back to the present.

"What?"

"Raul. He killed her. Celia. One of his putas. It was the locura, Paqo. She couldn't keep up with him. He washed up in front of my door one night covered in dirt and dripping in blood. A man possessed by esa locura can do anything, Paqo. I told him that he couldn't go to the police. That would've been the end of him. He wanted to go to your mother and ask her for help. I told him he was making a mistake."

Tía said it with such matter-of-factness. She didn't even lean in to tell me. I felt as though she was saying it more for herself. Her body as petrified as Tío's.

The air suffocated me when I stepped into the narrow corridor.

"There was so much blood . . . So much. I just didn't know what to do. So I helped him. We left her alone with only a canción de cuna. I sang it for her after we buried her . . . we took her to . . ."

I waited for her to finish. I wanted to know. But she didn't continue. She froze.

"You're the crazy one, Tía." I said, hoping it would trigger her to finish the story. She just sat there mesmerized by her own words, by Raul's casket.

I got up from her side and left her there. The air suffocated me when I stepped out into the narrow corridor. I scanned each registry as I glided by the podiums. Some of the rooms were vacant. I searched for Ma and Pa. You could hear the priests conducting sermons; the Catholic rites were dreary and melancholic. I wanted to cry but the tears wouldn't come. As if the priests were casting a counterspell that didn't let me have the release I needed. Their own fufú hurled onto me. Something was coming for me.

Outside, the mountains circled the cemetery. They encased the ridge where the cement plots rested, their marble crosses and Bible inscriptions warding off lingering spirits. Dark graying clouds, pregnant with rain, were speared by the green summits. The sun shone only on the isolated funeral home and cemetery. I started to get worried that Ma and Pa had run off on foot.

I stumbled to the far end of the parking lot. There was a large wooden shed hidden by many sprouting bamboos. Crickets screeched and a pair of changos pecked at some old garbage. Their jet-black feathers and hollow yellow eyes scanned my face. I crouched closer to them, closer to the pile of garbage they zealously grazed in. They pecked and dug out the remains of an old paloma; its guts were hooked on one chango's beak, the small intestine dangling like a bloody earthworm. The other chango tucked its entire head into the inflated breast of the paloma, in search of its heart. They were unmoved by my presence.

I could hear music—boleros—playing into the air. I squeezed through some of the tough dull husks of bamboo and tried glaring through the corroded window of the shed. It was too scratched up and clouded by moisture. I moved to the front of the shed, a large steel door was open. A young man's voice was singing with the radio.

> No amount of force lightning would move me elsewhere.

Something in me told me to go back. In Lares, the muse of El Grito can speak to you through the sounds caught on dry leaves. If the whistling cuts at you in such a way that cools every hair on your face, you know it's time to step. And if the muses of Ramón Emeterio Betances or Segundo Ruiz Belvis find you, the rain, which has only one allegiance—to continuity—will send you squirming back into your rathole. Like any good and defiant boy unblemished by that historical burden, I went against the breeze, against the gods, Atabey, and Emperor Palpatine himself. No amount of force lightning would move me elsewhere. I was terrified but I was drawn by the sway of the violin, the voice of the man. I poked my head into the space. There were stacks of Pinaud Clubman bottles lining the walls; their green glow mixed with the white excess talcum residue on the floor and gave the shed a pastel dusting. A long rack of black suit jackets and generic white shirts decorated the room's interior. And the bare bodies of dead men were piled next to each other on a silver surface.

A boy was dressing a young cadaver. He sang to the bolero in the backdrop and swayed his hips. He stuffed the dead body into a loose black jacket and powdered its stoic, gray face. He dabbed small amounts of powder on the body's thighs and dug out some makeup from a brown knapsack.

The dead body resisted the boy's attempt at moving it to another table, and I began to tear up. I felt my eyes heavy but the fufú cast by the priests didn't let me cry. I wished to feel closer to their synchronized steps.

The boy tussled with the dead body as he picked it up from the table and danced with it to the back of the room where the caskets were. The dead limbs flapped against the sides of the boy. He reached the crescendo of his hymn, his singing stirred the milky glass windows, and the shed shook with his voice.

He tried his best to find a spot in the shed that could hold the dead body upright. Then the boy caught my eyes and stopped humming to himself.

"You can't be in here, cabrón!" he barked at me. I didn't budge. The pale body was thin. And I could make out slits on the backs of its legs. They were calloused over and delicately manicured. Its forehead was cut in all sorts of places, as if a crown of thorns had been placed over its head.

"You hear? Get out!" He struggled with the weight of the body. The head snapped back and I saw its eyes glossed over, half open, shyly revealing themselves like pearls just excavated from a dirty clam. Its jaw opened and the bolero that scored the air was magnified. The same notes Felipe "La Voz" Rodriguez crooned. The dead told me to run. Far away from the spell. From that place. A storm was collecting. It was cold. A black mass caught in the cadaver's open mouth. I could only make out the patterns of feathers; black feathers compacted into one bulk and used as a microphone.

"Who was that? What happened to him?" I asked the boy.

"Get out, cabrón! You are going to get me in trouble. Get out!" the boy repeated and shouted and the dead shook in his embrace. Both of their mouths growing wider and wider and their voices trembling against every surface.

Until it suddenly all stopped.

The spell broke. I caught sensation in my toes and ran out of the shed and out through the small thicket of bamboos before running into the warm sun of the parking lot. The fat gray clouds were still stranded on the tips of the mountains. The pale body hung over me while its eyes kept shouting.

I found Ma seated on the crystal bench in front of the funeral home; the imposing cross stitched with the lettering NUESTRO DIOS cast a long shadow over her.

"Paqo, come here," she said to me. I rushed to her and sat on her lap, trying to force her to cradle my stiff body.

"Paqo, you're too old for that. You're too heavy. Get off. What would your father say," she shoved me from her lap and sat me next to her.

"You look like you've seen a fantasma, mijo."

I wanted to cry. To spark some sympathy from her. But the sun dried my eyes. I held my breath in hopes that she would notice my face scribbled with emotion but she didn't pay attention and kept asking about my clammy forehead. She petted my hair. She ran her sharp nails over the back of my neck to calm me down.

"Paqo. We have something to do. Something that'll help your Tío out. He needs guidance. We all do after we die."

"Ma. This place is haunted. This place is going to kill us. Tía Carmen says it's the locura. It's the curse."

"Don't say that. Pay respect," she swatted my forehead with the palm of her hand. "We are going to have to move him."

"Where?"

"Tía Carmen agreed to host el velorio."

"But why?"

"Because that is what he would've wanted. El velorio de familia. De casa."

"Why?"

"It's what he would've wanted." She paused. "To be close to family. To be close to you."

We were headed farther into the heart of Lares. To Tía Carmen's house. To witness Tío's heavy shell.

II. A DEAD SLEEPWALKER

La Iglesia Parroquia San José of Lares is the overseer of the town. It sits, plain and picturesque, on a central hill. Its tall domed bell tower tipped with a cross connects to the church's worship dome. Across from it in La Plaza Revolución, you have the giant bust of Ramón Emeterio Betances. Sculpted a bit ambitious as far as beards go. El cabrón was modeled more after Zeus than the moreno himself. His large head, the size of a cannon-ball, garnishes a cement Lares flag.

Walk farther away from the church and you'll come up to a fifteen-foot-tall cement obelisk painted in white and adorned with a fading copper plaque. The names of the Dons: Manuel Rojas, Venancio Román, Manolo El Leñero, Joaquín Parrilla, and company are there as evidence that something historical happened.

Pa was driving much slower than usual. His mind drifted.

"How are they bringing Tío to Tía Carmen's?" I asked.

The radio tuned to Zeta 93, Pa's boleros scored the car ride.

"Pa, do people grow older after they die? Pa, is Tío going to get wrinkled?"

"Take it easy, Paqo," Pa snapped.

"Pa, Tía said Tío Raul had locura. Why does she keep repeating that?"

"Leave it alone, Paqo."

"I just wanted to know." I began to draw on the car window with my finger, hoping to distract myself.

"Pa! I was thinking we could stop and get some helado. Please. Pa, I really want the carrot . . ."

"Cállate! We are only here for one reason. Not wasting time stuffing our faces."

A soft rain started thumping against the car. Ma turned her head toward him and pinched his hand.

She was protecting me from his canines. How he salivated at the chance to bite into my heart and teach me the proper ways of being a man. That something he wasn't telling me wanted release, wanted to see the air. But Ma, she grew larger and her eyes shimmered a yellow that shook the colors of the sun. She was trying to cover my potential scars with her black feathers.

> La Iglesia Parroquia San José of Lares is the overseer of the town.

"Pa, please."

"No!" He shouted. "I'm sick and tired of you, Paqo. You are no longer an only child. You need to stop con la inmaduréz and learn to think of others. There is no eating maldito ice cream during your . . . during your uncle's funeral."

"Take it easy, Ignacio," Ma jumped into the ring with her pecho paloma. Her voice shrilled as loudly as a chango's. "This isn't the place or time."

"Tu hijo needs to grow a pair. He has his head up his ass! Just like Raul . . ."

"Ignacio! Qué te pasa? Don't start this. Not now."

Pa pulled the car to the curb of the sinking road and parked. The rain started to fall harder. He opened the door and walked straight for the bush as if he needed to piss. I couldn't see him through the gray wetness. The windows of the Corolla were fogged. Ma turned to me.

"Don't worry, mijo. Your dad is just tired. He's resting. Yes"—she turned her head back to the front—"resting."

She opened the car door and stepped out into the falling rain. She left the door ajar and water soaked into the upholstery. The raindrops mimicked firecrackers going off into the air, each droplet grew louder as it started to plummet harder, Ma's open door magnifying the noise.

I tried moving in my seat. I didn't unbuckle my seat belt. After ten minutes Ma and Pa came back. They didn't speak to each other. They were drenched. Drops streamed down Ma's wet hair. Her breasts were visible through her white dress. Her legs were visible through her white dress. Pa shut his door and wouldn't drive off, rather he stayed staring at Ma without speaking. He finally set the car to gear and we drove to Tía Carmen's.

Tía Carmen was standing post when we pulled into her driveway. Her house was on tall zancos. The cars parked in the open first level between the cement stilts. The crumbling stairs that led to the main floor were slicked wet.

> "Was I supposed to buy your macho a home just to satisfy his spirit?"

She gave us a weak wave. Her large umbrella shielded her produced hair from the lather of rainwater.

"Nice shower, huh?" Tía said. "You should probably consider una sombrilla next time. They sell them at el colmado really cheap."

She started laughing. Pa stood over her, heavy with water.

"You could have showered here. We weren't going to charge you," she jested.

Ma lifted her wet finger up to Tía Carmen's face and walked up the crumbling stairs. I wanted to jump into the puddle next to Tía just to get her back. Pa read my mind. El viejo took me by the arm and dragged me into the house.

There, in the kitchen, was Tío Raul. Hanging loose in his casket. The veil concealed his face. His gray wig had been removed and was resting on one of the dining room chairs. Ma walked over to him and smiled. She placed her hand on his shoulder and leaned in and pecked him on the forehead. I wanted to laugh. But Ma was happier seeing Raul there, in his natural setting. And all his close friends seemed happier too.

There were two six-packs of Medalla and a crate full of cheap pinot grigio. Tía Carmen had pinned the original Puerto Rican flag in its baby-blue glory against a bare green wall. Next to it, the flag of Lares. And next to it, the good ol' American flag. How patriota of her. The hypocrisy of Tía Carmen. She did it as a joke. Because all of her actions revolved around keeping everything at least fifty degrees cooler than serious. The weight of those flags lined together, in that household where Raul would've gone full zombie and bitten Tía Carmen's brains out if he could. In that household, in that town, on this island. Yet even so, I felt an inclination, a desire to march right up to her and spit in her hair, to drop a nice thick gargajo so it could seep through that black mane. Must've been the ghost of Raul trying to act out his own frustrations through me. Ma's fufú.

"Take Paqo to his room, Ignacio," Ma said to Pa. Tía huffed and puffed up the stairs.

"There's no space for little Paquito in the bedrooms," Tía said flapping her arms like the wings of a pitirre. "We are all booked up for the night."

"You have to be kidding me, Carmen!" Ma barked at her. "You make us drive all the way here. You arrange Raul to have his rites done in the funeral home even though you knew it was supposed to be in his home. Somewhere he could be comfortable."

"Qué casa, Monsy? Hmm? Was I supposed to buy your macho a home just to satisfy his spirit? Should I go out and buy Paqo a new father too?"

"Carmen!" Ma shouted.

She started to fidget there, standing over me trying to shield me from Tía Carmen's venom.

"Ma?" I said. "What is she talking about?"

I tugged on her white dress. Carmen wore a long smirk on her face. Pa was scanning the floor, looking pathetic, pretending no one existed.

Ma grabbed my arm and dragged me into the bathroom. She shut the door behind us and propped herself up against the wall. And there it happened. She leaned into her knees and started crying. Her skirt wrinkled from its dampness. I'd never seen Ma break before.

"I'm sorry, Paqo."

"Ma, what's going on?"

Pa knocked on the door and inched it open.

"Monsy. Let's just spend an hour here. Then we'll leave."

"No. We need to stay."

"Ma?"

She tried swiping the streams from her face. She stood there crying but all I kept thinking about was the dead body. About fufú. About Raul.

After a minute she collected herself, took me by the hand, and walked us back to the living room, where Tía was now seated in her recliner like Jabba the Hutt.

"Can we stay, Carmen? We'll sleep on the floor. Paqo will sleep on the floor."

Tía let out a cough and grunted.

"Fine. Diego stays on the couch, though. He's come from Villalba. He needs rest for the drive back tomorrow."

"Okay," Ma conceded.

That night I couldn't sleep. Ma and Pa were wrapped in a red blanket the color of blood. I needed to use the bathroom but I didn't want to tiptoe through the darkness. A candle was lit at each end of Raul. The light did not spread evenly and the hallway's darkness was not extinguished. But I needed to pee. I crossed my legs hoping I could pinch the feeling away but I couldn't. I wiggled to my feet and made toward the bathroom.

Then came the scratch. I felt long nails cut into the back of my neck. I jumped in terror. Nothing. The candles flickered, then danced with each other. Raul's hands were elevated in his casket. I thought Tía was at it again. Another one of her ill-fated jokes.

A fear so cold and deep struck me. I kept remembering the strange songs that Ma used to chant as she cleaned our home in Santana. Hoping they were counterspells. Things she'd sing to protect us from evil. Not bothered by the possibility that they could've been, in fact, new curses, new parasites looking to feed. There I was, trying to run from a past that no one wanted to rediscover. Even if it was through a dead man. The only thing that brought me comfort was the hope that fufú, in its all-encompassing complexity, would save me.

Then Raul's hands twitched. I tried convincing myself that it was the movement of the candles. But the shadows that pierced out of the candlesticks were flat and still. And Raul's hands started to bend.

I was immoveable. The hallway was pitch black. All the doors from the bedrooms were shut.

"Hola?" I whispered. I expected a return *hello*. The fans in the living room circled over Ma and Pa. Each click as the dangling metal strings tapped against one another provided the only comfort.

"Hola?" I repeated. This time a little louder.

I saw him move his fingers again in the air. I felt pushed back against the wall with all the flags and watched as Raul trembled out of his casket. He pressed through the cotton veil. His eyes were an orange that stood out against the shadow of his outline. It couldn't be him! No way! I rubbed my eyes and pressed my back in retreat against the cool wall behind me. He swayed with every floating step and his hands extended in my direction.

I watched him inch closer. Sensation returned. I turned and bolted through the black hallway toward the bathroom. I locked the door and crawled into the dirty tub. It was grainy and there were patches of dark black and green mold all over the footing. It wasn't him, I repeated to myself. It wasn't him. All the damp and cold that anyone could consume, I was consuming it in the tub, curled and waiting for the heat of the morning sun. I wouldn't move from that position. It was the safest I had felt since before the boy danced with the pale dead body in the wooden shed of the cemetery. It had to have been the music. Fufú reborn.

I chanted as confidently as I could at the door. I slowly moved my lips as I waited for Raul to come through. That shadow transformed and I saw Pa in its dark drape. I wanted to dispel that power—his power—over me. To kill him.

Raul's hands were elevated in his casket.

I remembered Ma. How certain she was that Raul's spirit needed guidance. But our fufú chained us together, chained us to her and kept him grounded and uneasy. He became the changos pecking into the guts of the paloma. Into me.

Pa's knocking woke me.

"Paqo, open this door. There are people that need to use the bathroom. You are making everyone late," he said. I was drenched in water. Felt as though the ghost of Raul had sat on top of me the entire night. My skin was scrapped by the rust from the tub. The mold stained my shirt green.

"Paqo!" he repeated.

"Okay!" I shouted back. I opened the door and the entire crew was standing there.

"You take a shower all night?" Tía asked.

"Paqo. Why are you wet?" Ma asked.

I poked my head out of the bathroom door, scanning the kitchen. Raul's casket was shut, the white veil folded over its center.

"He's there, he's awake," I said.

"Qué?" Tía asked.

"Raul. Is . . ."

"He's dead, mijo. The dead don't walk. They don't need to," she responded.

"Vamos, Paqo. Let's get you dressed," Ma interrupted. She took me by the hand but I yanked back.

"Ma, he was walking. He was. Last night. He got out of there." I pointed at the casket. "He used the light from the candles as a channel. A way out."

"Paqo. Y esta locura?" Tía said. She put her hand over her mouth and tried holding back a laugh. It burst open and she started cackling, then coughing. Then cackling. It was true Huttese. I wanted to cry. Every person there was eyeing me with their judgment. Este niño. Este loco.

"Carmen!" Ma yelled. "Don't!"

Me, the fallen Solo frozen in carbonite, and Ma, the rescuing pincess.

"Nena, cálmate. He's a tough kid. Even if he's picked up some of his father's locura."

She leaned against the wall of her house with the same confidence as Jabba. Ma broke. She stomped toward her. In front of everyone. She smacked her across her face, the snap rung through the entire house and chimed off the plates in the kitchen, off the metal stirring spoons and pots that were latched and hanging on the ceiling rack near dead Raul.

Tía wiped the shame from her cheek. In disbelief that Ma would be so bold as to embarrass her in front of all her people. It was the same reaction you'd expect from a child reprimanded in front of all the cool kids. She patted her cheek without saying a word to Ma. Ma didn't need to say anything to her. Pa acted as if he hadn't seen a thing. He walked up to me and grabbed my small hand and escorted me out.

III. TREADING WATER

A couple of days after the burial, Pa received a call. We were in Santana. We hadn't left the house because by some galactic force, the tropical depression that was supposed to come and go decided to camp out over the entire island. Puerto Rico was on terminal lockdown and the flood warnings were buzzing through our transistor radio. It was unexplainable—Noticentro had a field day covering the mayhem.

> Puerto Rico was on terminal lockdown and the flood warnings were buzzing through our transistor radio.

Ma was rocking Yamil on her lap. He coughed and smiled as Ma blew on his stomach. He let out these tiny growls. I wanted to hit Yamil. I felt like hurting him.

"Monsy," Pa said into her ear. It was so quiet in our home, I heard every word he spoke. "Carmen called. We need to rush to Lares. We need to rush to el cementerio."

He moved his lips over Yamil's forehead and gave him a soft kiss. Then he let out a commanding whistle at me, the same shriek from the funeral home.

"Now? Ignacio, it's impossible to drive in this," Ma said.

"It's bad. We need to go."

She hesitated. Yamil tugging on her dangling silver hoop earing.

"Okay. Let me call Ramona."

Ma treated our Yamil with such delicacy. Pa moved in to smother him. He kissed his small hands and grinned whenever he let out tiny chuckles. Ma waited an entire hour until Doña Ramona—our neighbor—came to babysit Yamil before we jetted off in the Corolla.

Rain and rain. We saw the clay slide from the side of the mountains like from a pierced gut, the green banks bleeding out thick red rivers of mud. Pa knew the danger in driving yet he still pushed forward, Zeta 93's boleros soothing him through the haze with the screech of trumpets. Ma frequently turned to me and smiled as reassurance. Her smiles bothered me. I wasn't scared. Maybe because I too wanted to know. I needed to see it. In the vortex outside, I saw the changing of season; I saw how the raw trees that wanted to withstand the deluge needed to bend and mold together, the men on the sides of the road pleading for help. The houses clogged with water and the women holding high above their heads their farmed yucca and ramos de platano. They scrounged to find any possible fruit of their labor, trying to save anything that could be sold later. Even though they knew it was all going to be washed away, they still tried.

"We should turn back, Ignacio," Ma whispered to him. "No creo que vale la pena."

"We're almost there," he said. "We need to help them if they need it."

"Okay, okay," she said.

"Pa, hurry!"

"Ya, Paqo. Leave your father alone. We are trying . . ."

"Pa! Hurry! Pa! Hurry!"

They didn't respond. We kept crawling up the mountain. I started chanting to myself, chanted all possible incantations and soon felt my eyes glow. Maybe it was more about performance. The sound of the changos plucking into the dead pigeons, the screech of the violins from the bolero, the growing thunder and wind collecting outside.

"Paqo?" Ma said.

I ignored her and chanted louder hoping they all heard me, hoping Raul heard my song.

I could make out the church at the center of town. I could see the cemetery and the cars parked along the sides of the thin road because they could not see in front of them. Our Corolla inching closer to the slanted gates of the cemetery. The bamboos snapped outside, a cluster of them bent so far down, the green tips swept the roof of the car.

We reached the edge of the hill, and the entrance to the cemetery gates was closed off. A Mack truck blocked the road and two National Guard MTVRs blended in with their green calico patterns against the mountain backdrop. Pa parked next to one of the trucks and got out. My chants reduced to an inconsistent mumble.

You could make out Tía's fat body in the gray setting. I watched Pa and Tía there. Ma watched them. They spoke with one of the uniformed men. Their hands flailed in the air. Pa then pointed to the cemetery. They all looked in that direction. I wanted to get out and see but Ma must've felt my impulse and reached her hand back. She affectionately tapped my knee. Cool down. Cool off. Her eyes met mine and she let out a forced smile.

He returned to us as expected, sagged by the water that collected on his jeans. He tapped on Ma's window and she rolled it down.

"They are out. It's bad, Monsy," he said. "The rain broke them and now there's a mess."

"What are they planning on doing?" she asked.

"Right now, they can't do anything until the rain stops."

"So what do we do now, Ignacio?"

"Stay here. Best to hold on to your last images as long as you can. You don't want to see any of this."

It didn't matter that I would get soaked. It wasn't as if the water would melt you if you stepped into it. I felt the voice of Raul chanting in my ears and his extended hands, his shadow pushing me against Tía's wall a few nights before. How I hid from the world in that porcelain tub waiting for sleep to take me because I knew Raul would get me. It was all reflex, a jolt in my fingers that pulled out the lock of my passenger door. I opened it.

"I want to see, Pa," I said.

"NO! Listen to me, mijo! Close that door."

"I want to see, Pa," I repeated.

"Listen to me! I am your father . . ."

I started kicking my feet against the seat.

"Stay in the car, Paqo. Monsy, grab your son."

"Ma, I want to see!" I repeated.

"Cálmate, Paqo. Everything will be all right. Hold on to me. Everything will be fine." She grabbed my foot before I could sling my body out of the car.

"Let go, Ma! I want to see!" I flailed my foot in the air, a fish desperate to return to water, desperate to feel the moisture run through my coarse hair and my dark skin lathered by its soft coldness.

"Paqo!" Pa yelled.

He ran around the car in an attempt to stop me. I loosened my shoe and fell to the ground. I hit my shoulder on the watery asphalt; the splash of water met my face, the particles of sand and mud mixed into my hair. Pa helped me up from the ground. Ma got out of her seat and rushed to me in panic.

And there he was: Raul. He had escaped his wooden home and was swimming down the banks of the mud river.

"Paqo. You are all right. You are all right," she said and bear-hugged me. She tried petting me, clawing her nails down my spine, but I shook her off me.

I thought Pa would flip into a fit of anger but he didn't. He picked out some of the grains and small rocks from my head.

We stood there, drenched, as if posing for a family portrait. The rain didn't let up. We watched as the National Guard worked in their sodden clothes, the weight of water slowing down their movements. They tried shoving some of the plant debris off the road. You could see the entire cemetery, every fissured grave, every plot and oval prayer circle, every alabaster mausoleum crumbled or crumbling by the wayside. The ground had split right down the middle of all the colorful plots. The black marble crosses that crowned the graves were cracked. Some of the heavy cement slabs that were meant to cover the tombs where the caskets dwelled were removed and shattered down the ledge of the pouring mountainside. You could see the tubing from the ground that was designed to drain excess water; its exposed lines were bleeding veins from a severed limb.

But the caskets. Some were floating on the makeshift lake that grew and grew as the water fell. And there were cadavers. Neatly dressed with their guayaberas or black suits strewn atop gravesites, atop the brown and red mud and blended with the uprooted trees. Some were tossed down the side of the mountain in maladjusted positions; the head of an older large woman was bent backward and her thin, long, and gray hair was woven with the roots of a fallen tree. It looked as if she were being hung.

And there he was: Raul. He had escaped his wooden home and was swimming down the banks of the mud river, no longer wearing the prized wig that was bought to make him appear younger. His thin hands stroked the rain all mariposa, or freestyle. His head took two more breaths before he reached the edge of the cemetery, where the land splintered into two divides. Pa grabbed me and tried covering my eyes. But I pushed him away. I ran.

"Paqo! Paqo, get back here!" Ma started pleading. I didn't listen. I jumped from one cracked grave onto the next. The men in uniform watched me as I dodged the crosses that scatted by me with the water. The plastic flowers that were glued onto cement urns littered the muck with blue and pink artificial colors. I wanted to catch one last sight of him before he was gone. Raul's head turned to me and shook as the brown mud started covering all his body, his dark skin and pampered suit became petrified with the brown mud and tangled roots. His eyes glowing yellow before the thick moving river covered him. All fufú washed away. He tumbled down the ridge into the forested valley, and every shattered cement slab, every adorned cross, the logs and roots and pipes of bamboos fell over him. He disappeared. 🜛

Gabrielle Calvocoressi

AFFIRMATION CISTERN I LOVE AND TEND MY ONE AND ONLY BODY

Though it's hard and ticklish work,
I sweep the forests with my feet.
Making little pyres of the pinecones.
Little cairns. I wash the faces
of the rocks with my hands and sometimes
also with my tongue. No fooling!
I am trying to appreciate the body.
My body. I open my ear holes
so I can feel the tunnel from birdsong
to my root. I'm trying not to want
too much. If I come upon the bones
of an animal: a squirrel, say,
or a raccoon, I try to feel it
in my body. I try to be quit of the earthly
idea that I am not sibling to a squirrel
or a raccoon. Try to strip away
notions of dominion I learned
in some book. I shine its little
dead teeth and don't take them
for a necklace or some possibility
of a weapon to kill another person with.
I let all the bleached femurs

of every animal remain where they
fell. And I think, *That's what I'd want.*
My femur, my jaw, the empty
gong of my pelvis allowed to rest
and not be put to work again.
If some other animal wants
to build a castle out of cricket
shells and badger sternums,
that's cool. But maybe I'll
just leave the bones alone.

NOBILITY CISTERN WE HAVE STALWART FRIEND

There were more dark corridors
on this planet than I could fathom.
Everywhere, a dark corridor. In the
houses for sleep and the houses for
healing. In the God houses. In the
skin houses that cooed and bludgeoned
and sometimes both at once. So many
dark places. And always something
coming to find you when you just
wanted some privacy. Even the dinner
plate had its dark corners. So even
my food wasn't my own. Where
did it come from? The arm and then
darkness and all my chicken casserole
and vegetables gone.

You could get killed for not passing
the salt. You could get killed for not
saying good morning. You could get
every bone in your body broken
because you didn't bring in the paper,
didn't keep the woodstove burning,
didn't get the ball in the basket. No.
It was a joke. I was supposed to be
laughing.

A good way to know was how they
treated their animals. I lay awake
in my light body and heard the wooden
pointer whistling through the air
until it hobbled the dog. Into my light body:
her light body whimpering. Cowered.
But then licking the forearm. Then running
along the riverbanks beside it.

Sometimes I'd hit the dog too. With the newspaper
rolled tight into a log. Hollow. Hollow drum of her flank.

My head hung with her forehead resting on mine.

dear baba, you tell me you had to leave because you cannot speak here, that in karachi you have a tongue again. baba, i have been losing words. this morning i woke up and there were all these words that went missing. baba, what is the word for *longing* in urdu? baba, teach me how to write my name again.

baba, do not leave me in this city where my skin feels lost. what about me, baba? where do i run to? where is the land that reaches out to me, calls me child? where my tongue can speak without betrayal? the urdu is disappearing, baba, from my mouth and my fingertips.

baba, must the children of diaspora dream of homelands only in poetry? are we scattered seeds that will never take root? baba, my generation is giving up on the notion of home. yesterday, a fellow child of diaspora looked at me through a computer screen and confessed with red eyes, *you are my home.* baba, maybe we are each other's homes and maybe that is enough. maybe we need to hold each other across oceans and speak tenderness in our broken languages.

dear baba, i have little tolerance for people who are sticklers for grammar. i think it's because you always asked me to edit your emails. waited every day for me to come home and make sure your response to the craigslist ad was professional and correct, and i kept telling you it doesn't matter. don't make it matter. baba, why is it that centuries after their invasion we still cannot shake off the trauma of white supremacy? if trauma can be inherited, so can racism. and rebellion. the white colonizers never learned my language half as well after they invaded and plundered us, and then fed insecurities into our bloodstreams. why must we try so hard?

baba, i write in english because it is what i have, but i will break it. i will break this
language, pull it open and tuck in phrases too foreign. mera wada he. i promise to
write in bad grammar and not speak all good and misspell in every craigslist email
and every school assignment i can get away with. i will place at least one intentional,
seditious error in all my assignments. just for us, baba.

baba, it has been raining for weeks. i wish i could send some over to you. i remember
the word for *rain*. barish. *ba rish*. The pause of *ba* as the monsoon clouds loom.
rish, relief felt as water kisses parched land. the way the entire city smells like rain.
karachi knows the poetry of rain. the way we ran onto the roof, our heads upturned,
mouths open for the first drops of water. do you remember when chachu sent me an
umbrella from america and i took it to the roof after spotting a gray cloud? i waited
for hours under my american umbrella. i have never seen anyone use an umbrella in
karachi, baba. i wonder if that has changed or whether the neighborhood children
still swarm onto the streets, heads skyward, anticipating the first rain drop.

dear baba, there is no word for *des* in english. *nation? homeland?* no, not quite. english cannot
fully comprehend its own oppression. you are my des, baba. call me when it rains. i
remember the word for it. *barish*. taste of rain on my tongue. barish on my zaban.

PROMETEO

The cane field owns you. You own the cane field.
You never stole fire, you created it.

∞

A convex or flat bevel, from spine to edge,
a secondary bevel to have a slight distal taper—
resistant to chipping and breaking,

the blade must be tempered not heat-treated
the way common knives are. It stands up to
repeated impacts. It does not easily break if abused.

∞

Nothing is ever as simple as it appears.
You know this. Whether held by the farmer
or the guerilla, your clean, sharp surface
is but an extension of the arm.
How many times have men tried to make
of you a symbol only to fail?

∞

My father cleared an acre quicker than
a machine with nothing more than a machete.

∞

When you speak to us, you
speak Español—but you are
fluent in Armenian, Malaysian,
Thai, Portuguese, Tagalog,
and numerous languages
from the African continent.

∞

Weapon of choice for uprisings, we so desired you
we adopted your name, became Macheteros.

∞

I imagine the carbon springs to life under the hammer,
the edge sharpened to starshine. Striking rock with it
kindles fires, its sparks numerous and bright.
There was always fire within the machete.

∞

Strange inheritance, one I denied for so long.
I listen to you daily even though you say little.
Next to you, I can still smell the fire of sugar.

See You

Annie really had wanted to learn the drums; that wasn't bullshit. She had her reasons: release some rage, tone her arms, look cool. Also they'd just signed the papers—he'd taken the bookshelves, she'd kept the debt—and distraction seemed wise. Drums offered both math and catharsis; she could rely on the first, mend with the second.

Katie Arnold-Ratliff

But then she paid the music school for twelve lessons, twice assured by the receptionist that she wasn't the only student older than twelve, and when a confirmation email arrived bearing her teacher's photo, Annie saw that he was monstrously cute. He had mussed hair, and the dulcet, crinkle-eyed expression women read as evidence of decency. And so her reasons changed.

She saw the potential in seconds. How nice when life handed you just what you needed. She'd wade through the swamp of this divorce by bedding her teacher, reinvigorating herself, before jettisoning him to pursue her destiny. The twinning of drums and sex was natural, simple: all that rhythmic throbbing before crescendo. One rudiment was called the diddle, for God's sake. Her man-child teacher would teach her drums, and she would teach him the art of grown-up fucking. She had a catalog of stern, sexy commands to draw from, was practiced in telling boys what to do. They all wanted to be told what to do.

OMG, texted Mimi, her friend of some decades.

I know, Annie replied. *It's perfect. It's too perfect.*

You're so lucky, Mimi said, because she, like everybody, had been broken by love.

On lesson day, in the music school's lobby, all seemed in order: her teacher seemed stunned at the sight of her, and his hand was humid when she shook it.

Hi, hey, he said, *what's up. I'm Joey.*

He wore the constricted smile of the shy, a seafoam T-shirt that veed between the contours of his chest, unbelted black jeans, ratty sneakers. He was pudgy, only just, with a skittish mumble and a bearing like that of a scolded dog, a rare boy unaware that good looks entitled him to saunter around sucking up goodwill. Yet his diffidence didn't prevent him from staring at Annie as he walked her down the hall—he smacked his elbow on a bulletin board shingled with flyers—and as they passed a soundproof glass chamber lined with gleaming guitars, and as they descended the stairs to the drum room, and also for a mute, decelerated moment once they entered it.

Let's warm up, he said.

He sat her at a kit and took his place at one facing her, watchful as a cat.

So go ahead and just start hitting stuff, he said. *Like, just rage out.*

She lifted the sticks, then sat there paralyzed. *I can't?*

He paused, perhaps waiting to see if she was kidding.

Fair enough, he said, glancing away. *No worries.*

Wait, she said. She wasn't someone who failed. She smacked the hi-hat, unaware of its pedal; wide open, it coughed up a woozy rattle. She bonked the rack tom, producing a rubbery echo. She coaxed a puny thump from the bass drum, her tibialis weak. She met his eyes, pained.

Okay, he said.

But so what. Only a minor dip in momentum, because look how he was looking at her again—as if she wasn't real, as if she were a trick—and smiling involuntarily with every tenth word.

She didn't notice at first how young he was. No, wait—she did notice he was so young, she just forgot she wasn't. For days afterward she thought, in the non-thought way she not-thought about lots of things, they were roughly the same age. Annie was old enough to feel youth's ceiling bruising her head—could hear it crack, plaster littering her hair—but in her mind was still like twenty-four, perpetually post-adolescent. Then she rooted around a social network until she saw her teacher graduating from college in a photo dated not two years prior, and got mired in cruel equations: *He was in high school when I was in grad school. He was in third grade when I went on birth control. He was legit born in the nineties.*

> She only ever called him, in her head and in texts to Mimi, The Drummer.

She only ever called him, in her head and in texts to Mimi, The Drummer.

First, he taught Annie a softball song, satisfyingly ride-thrashing, to entice her, then moved on to scores of undemanding cross-arm beats she was to play in ruminative loops. He wanted her to start at the beginning, to be a beginner, which Annie resented. He wanted her to learn rudiments: rolls, drags, flams, dragadiddles, paradiddles, flamacues, ratamacues, pataflaflas, so she'd have a nimble repertoire of moves with which to improvise (or *jam*, which was an actual word he actually used).

I'll never be able to put in the ten thousand hours, she told him. *Like, just FYI. But I'm fine with being a mediocre drummer.*

Mediocrity can take you pretty far in drumming, he said. *It's not an instrument that rewards virtuosity.*

He greeted her the same way each lesson—*How's your week, what's been going on?*—and after she said, *Not much, you?* and he said, *Doing good*, fighting his panicky smile, all he talked about was the 808 or the German grip or Ringo draping tea towels over his toms or her many, many mistakes.

You're still driving the stick into the snare, he said again and again.

He didn't praise her, even when she fished.

But then one night just as they finished he said, rapid-fire as an auctioneer, *After this I have to go find a costume, my band is playing this show and everybody dresses up, I always go as a hot dog but I feel I should branch out.*

Don't get crazy now, Annie said. *Maybe take it slow, go as a hamburger.*

The week after, he told her he'd gone as a hot dog in a bow tie: *I felt it said what I needed to say.*

The Deadpan Drummer, Mimi said. *The Little Drummer Boy, cracking jokes and looking down your shirt when you adjust a pedal.*

> Some people were well spoken but illiterate, it was survivable.

· · ·

She needed him to write out the notes, once he taught her to read music—needed to squint at the page as she drummed, because she couldn't play by ear or feel. He was patient when she cursed after an errant strike. She wasn't someone to make a scene of herself, but frequently some inner mechanism would malfunction and she'd act a damn fool. Once, frustrated, she threw her sticks. Once, she lifted her sticks too deliberately for a flam and whacked the bony hoop of her eye socket.

By lesson seven, she was itchy. This was taking too long. Two months had passed and she was no closer to him, to her empowered rebounding. So she created a plan: she'd write to Joey to request music recommendations, having found his email address on his band's frowzy website. She didn't need the recommendations, of course; the point was that her note would relocate their shared patter from the dank drum room to the world beyond it.

Smart! said Mimi. *He's shy, help him out!*

Annie sent the email on a Monday and for hours acted (for whom?) as though each time she checked her inbox it wasn't solely for his response. Which never came. It just never came. What the fuck now? Cement her disadvantage with a sad follow-up? Attend her remaining lessons as if nothing had happened? Hell no. She'd eat the money, call it a wash, invent for Mimi a less humiliating story about how it all ended that Annie would, in time, remember as truth. She sat on the office toilet on Tuesday, ignoring a pile of work, wondering. If not this—if not sex as salve—then what?

A text came: *Meet at Bering & Bering tomorrow, 4pm. Another doc to sign, insurance stuff.* She stared hard at her husband's name. How many times had she said it in all those years? A thousand, a million—she wasn't great with numbers.

If not this, what? If not him, whom? If not now, when?

What would happen to her? That was the question.

On Wednesday Joey replied.

It's great to hear from you I've enjoyed teaching you! Here is few ideas off top of my head.

Right, okay, bumbling diction was a bummer but not a deal breaker, some people were well spoken but illiterate, it was survivable, as was the fact that he'd listed three records Annie and everyone else her age already owned, inescapable in 2003, 2005, and 2008, which was when she was in college and newly married and then unhappily married. At first she was offended: Did Joey think she lived under a rock? *Oh, right,* she thought. He was a child then. He hadn't been sentient for these bands in real time; while she was sneaking spliffs into their shows he'd been learning geometry and getting his orthodontia torqued.

See you in a few days, he wrote, and then signed his little name.

And then, like some gift, he emailed again three days later, the surprise of it a strange luxury. *I don't know if your done with the lessons you paid the school for but I teach private lessons in my studio.*

The price he quoted was half market rate, such a modest proposal she pitied him. Then she got it. He was making her an offer she couldn't refuse. He was begging. Forget the school! She would lose money, she had paid them in advance, but this was worth it.

Shall we do it? he wrote when she didn't answer fast enough. *Another good thing is that there are mics there so I can sing along while you play which is helpful when your learning even though it stresses me out to sing in front of people haha.*

Let's do it, Annie wrote. *And I won't judge your singing, dude.*

You say that now haha, he wrote.

He gave her his number. *Text me,* he wrote. *I'll let you in.*

See you then, she wrote.

See you, he wrote.

Annie thought about Joey that night when she listened to the song in which the lady drummer halts her every dizzying fill into sudden nothingness, a cacophony that dies on a dime. It was the song that had made Annie want to learn the drums. Oh, right: the drums. Oh, right: her rosy baby boy of a drum teacher. What was he doing right now? It felt nice to wonder. The wondering was a buoy in her chest.

· · ·

Annie never visited this part of Brooklyn, where the L met the M and the twee charm of the borough's elsewheres was not in evidence. Little light reached the side streets, and the row houses were colorless in the dark, and rats strolled coolly across the pavement, and garbage cans were chained to wrought-iron stoop railings. When he swung open the door Joey greeted her like a man possessed:

Hey! he said. *It's good to see you!*

She couldn't answer for all his beaming.

Come on in, he said.

The "studio" was a squalid basement. Above Joey's comely mother-of-pearl kit hung a bare bulb. Once her eyes adjusted Annie noted a jug of Stoli atop an orange amp, a homemade sign on the wall that read THE ROAD TO HELL IS PAVED WITH GOOD INTENTIONS, a whiteboard bearing a scribbled set list. The sheet on the nearby futon still betrayed a body's impression, like the dented soil left by an excavated fossil. A human person lived here. It smelled like burning ass. A blond pit bull looked up at Annie: *You're staying?* his expression said. She went to pet him but he turned, and the pad of her thumb gored his eye. He leaned his head against her leg like a child, and she thought about how easily he could kill her.

Joey searched Annie's face. She hid her disgust as best she could.

So this is your place?

He shook his head, and she liked him again. *No, we practice here.*

She heard water running, and then an unshaven lad emerged from the bathroom. Joey made reluctant introductions and Annie instantly forgot Homeboy's name, just smiled and took her place at the kit and tried to ignore the briefs on the floor, balled beside a kids-meal box stuffed with condom wrappers. Then Homeboy left and it was just Annie, Joey, and the dog, which perched on the bottom step, watching. She warmed up with some accented triplets, studying Joey's back as he untangled a snake pit of mic cords.

Watch that left hand, he said, prying open a folding chair and sitting beside her. *Don't dig into the snare.*

She stopped, bored now with everything but his proximity.

What would you like to learn? he said.

What you taste like. What your parents do. Your home address.

There's all kinds of stuff we can try, Joey said. To him, music was a sonic buffet. *Try this Hendrix track*, he'd told her a few weeks prior, starting the stereo, *you'll learn about subdivisions of three.* Then he switched artists. *We could do this dance one, to put both hands on the hi-hat. Or this rap song*—he changed the track—*to learn half beats.*

That had all sounded nice, but Annie rarely practiced and was pretty terrible at playing the drums. *We could finish that song we started at the school,* she said: the hip-hop one she'd mostly aced, minus a thorny intro.

Fine, he said. *Show me what you remember, yeah? Onnne, twooo, threee, go—*

She settled into the beat, drawing it on the air, and he nodded along a moment, then walked toward the other end of the room. The glow from the bulb above her didn't reach far, and after a few steps she couldn't see him. She felt him watching

The sheet on the nearby futon still betrayed a body's impression, like the dented soil left by an excavated fossil.

her from his shadowed vantage. He materialized holding a dusty black bass, taking his place beside a mic stand. He began to pluck out the song's depths, the tremor from the orange amp rattling her sneaker soles. After a measure he launched shrilly into the lyrics. He was bad, but he let her hear. She couldn't think while playing—a thought of any kind, even about not having thoughts, stilled her hands. But tonight she did think, eyeing his mouth, and somehow her wrists kept moving. The thought was *This is a good way to learn who someone is.*

At the bridge he palmed the fretboard to halt things.

That was fun, she said.

Do you sing? he asked.

No, she said.

No, you're too timid for that.

She crossed her sticks in her lap, stung.

You gotta play with conviction, he said. *I pride myself on hitting the drums really hard, that's something that's, like, important to me. I draw on this well of aggression, like, rrrrrrgh.* He grimaced, lifting his fists to his middle.

You're thinking about actual stuff that angers you?

No, he said. *It's more abstract than that.*
A well of aggression. I'm sure I have one.
Use it, he said.

. . .

Things were feeling good, charged and inevitable, ascendant. And so Annie pledged to do the unthinkable: ask him out. That is, she'd ask, when he texted to set up her next lesson, if he wanted to *grab a beer after*. Annie had vetoed *have drinks* and *go for a bite* and settled on the boy-friendly *grab a beer after*, had obtained buy-in from Mimi re *grab a beer after*.

> *Hey! Lesson tomorrow at 8?* Joey texted.
> *For sure. Want to grab a beer after?*

A read receipt, that chit of acknowledgment—surely he didn't know his were enabled, surely not—told her he had seen this. A minute passed. Two. Texts required prompt answers; if she wanted to wait she'd have sent a fucking postcard. Three minutes. Four.

In the office bathroom stall Annie mashed her temple against the bisque partition, listening to the chorus of pee. She already knew. If Joey replied it'd be with a feeble fart of an excuse, just courteous enough to keep her as a customer. Man he wished he could but he had band practice, oral surgery, car trouble. She knew this. Why, then, had she asked? Because a parasite in her brain compelled her to do debasing, pointless things. It was called hope.

It occurred to her now that the only man who'd ever loved her, the one she'd just divorced, had also been the only man ever to chase her. Everyone else, from grade school to grad school, had been forced to hold the line as Annie plowed into them, head down, declaring her attraction with propositions masked as jokes, libidinous non sequiturs, soppy letters. Some liked her boldness; they received ever more potent doses of it until they didn't like it anymore. Some disliked her boldness; they received ever more potent doses of it until they disappeared. Annie would helpfully explain why the boy was wrong for not liking her back, offering a multipart plan for rectifying this error.

She was practiced in telling men what to do.

> ### She was practiced in telling men what to do.

They all wanted to be told what to do?

Perhaps, she thought, she'd treated romance like a calf-roping competition long enough that some stain of grasping officiousness would forever remain on her, impervious to reform. And she'd tried to be better, she really had. In these post-divorce months she'd been retiring and coy, nursing crushes, sewing closed her mouth, and still men fell away, repelled by a defect she suspected they'd be hard pressed to name. However quiet she kept it, her interest sickened them. Bent double on the office toilet, her forehead pinkening against her knees, Annie recalled the bearded ESL instructor who told her he'd written her an ardent email he hadn't had the courage to send, and when she asked, *What did it say?*, he snapped, *That's the last time I tell you anything.* And also the banker, he smelled so expensive, who drove her home beneath the GWB's grass-green glow and idled outside her apartment, groaning that he wanted her, that she was the only person with whom he could be himself, that he could tell she'd be *masterful, a hellcat*—and how, after he'd tented his gabardine slacks, she'd said, *So come find out*, and he'd sputtered, *That's a bad idea.* Plus the slim, serious guy who worked in marketing or something, what is marketing exactly, who kissed her collarbone at the table and bought her a Scotch older than she was and said, *Let's go to my place*, where on his couch she'd let her knee touch his—and how he pulled away so pitilessly she'd lost her wind. He'd stared out the window as she called herself a car.

Up to this moment, up to *grab a beer after*, Annie had vowed not to invite any more humiliation. How much could a person stand? And now she'd broken her promise and found the dating world to be as she'd left it: inhospitable and baffling.

She wiped her dumb, weepy face. Annie's eye makeup—she needed lots to be pretty—tracked the toilet paper as if she were shitting out of her eyeballs. She was thirty-six years old. Her triumph, her sexy salve, her salvation, were dots in the rearview.

She returned to her desk. Joey had answered *grab a beer after* after six minutes—*Sure yeah sounds good*—and she'd spent forty filling a toilet with tears.

Great, Annie said.

See you, he said.

Think of a measure like a typewriter, Joey said at her next lesson. *The cymbal is the, you know, that thing*—he swiped his hand across his solar plexus, returning an invisible carriage—*the thing that means you're starting a new line.*

The atmosphere oozed. Beer after. Beer after. *Grab a beer after.* He wore a plaid button-down, not a T-shirt. He'd gotten a haircut and smelled like shower. He tapped a stick against his lip, eyes darting. Boyish nerves, like lady-catnip! The dog rested his face on his lethal paws, lying on the futon. Annie whipped her wrist at the hi-hat, TACK-tink, TACK-tink, accenting alternating notes, here in the drumgeon of balled tissues and mossy ashtrays, here amid this mouse-in-the-walls stench.

Then time was up and the air pressure spiked, and Joey said, *How 'bout that drink?* as he investigated his dress shoes, oh shit dress shoes, like a kid on Easter.

He chose the bar, steering them through the soupy late-July air without a whiff of the pass-agg horseshit to which Annie's husband had always subjected her: *Where do you want to go, babe, you pick, up to you.* There was muscle in Joey choosing, a clipped manliness she prayed was foretelling. They shuffled down the parbaked sidewalk, passing drippy tags on cement walls and decaying midsize cars queued up like some turd parade. At the bar, a beer tap jutted from the belly of a topless, headless, armless mannequin, a torso bleeding Pacifico, which is what he ordered for them, gallantly handing the barkeep twelve dollars from the sixty Annie had just paid him. He collapsed onto the padded bench and left her the rigid wood chair, his cheeks pink as though he'd been boiled. His leg trembled. It alarmed her how scared he was: it might be contagious.

I have a tendency to ask a million questions, she said.

'*Kay,* he said.

Where are you from? A rich corner of north Jersey. *Did you like it there?* Shrug, smile. *What do your parents do?* Dad's a doctor, Mom's a dentist. *Is that why you have bad handwriting and good teeth?* Shrug, smile. *Where'd you go to school?* Columbia. *What'd you study?*

Psychology, Joey said. *I want to be a therapist. I have to go to grad school, but I'm not*—his eyes scurried, he was rushing to explain—*in a hurry to do that.*

You needn't be. I mean, how old are you?

Twenty-five, he said.

Do you have a roommate?

Two, actually.

Are they your age?

I think they're closer to your age.

Vicious, choking silence.

Do you go to therapy? Annie asked.

Joey blinked. *Yeah.*

Me too. Where would I be without it, I wonder. Dead, probably, haha. The words climbed her larynx like vomit. *And the medication . . .* She couldn't finish this sentence; she didn't know how it ended.

His voice was soft. *What do you take?*

She told him: two drugs daily, one as needed. *For depression, just boring old depression. What do you take?*

Lithium, he said.

Her brain flashed with the memory of something sharp and familiar, a montage of scenes she did not want to see.

You're bipolar, she said. Then she thought better. *You have bipolar disorder.*

The waitress sailed toward their table. *Another round?*

They ignored her until she backed away.

How'd you know? he asked.

She answered, and he asked how long ago they had divorced.

What her husband put her through, his illness, was something Annie didn't speak of. She didn't know why her mouth was doing this thing, this talking thing. What did it want?

I've thought of more questions, she said.

Go, he said.

When did you start learning the drums? At thirteen. *Was your teacher strict?* Not especially. *Did you like that movie about the strict drum teacher?* Not especially. *Do you have siblings?* Yes. *Did you grow up religious?* I'm Jewish, I guess. *Do you believe in God?* I believe that if there is a God, human beings wouldn't be able to comprehend him, that the form of God, the shape, would be beyond our understanding.

Oh, she said.

Do you believe in God?

Only residually, Annie said. *I grew up Christian. It never really goes away.*

When I was at the catacombs in Paris, Joey said, *there was this group of Christian teenagers, and one turned to the other and said, "I wish my family were here to see this with me!" which struck me as a very Christian thing to say.*

She laughed, and he did too, and it was the first time he ever had in front of her. It widened his face and made his teeth small. He looked like a different boy.

> You're bipolar, she said. Then she thought better. You have bipolar disorder.

She'd never been to Paris. She'd never been anywhere.

Was it really bad when you were depressed? he asked.

Her grin eroded. *Yeah,* she said. *Awful. What was it like when you were manic?*

Awful for everyone else, Joey said. *But great after being depressed. You know?*

Yes, she said. The beer was fizzing her brain. *When I'm depressed it's like a parallel me lives inside me, and she wants to kill me, and all she talks about, all day every day, in my voice, are the reasons why I deserve to die.*

He nodded, his nonchalance a relief.

What was it like when you were depressed? she asked.

He leaned in. His breath smelled of beer's watery wheat. *It was like I had no soul. Everyone was walking around with souls but I didn't have one.*

I've never talked about this stuff with a person I wasn't paying, she said.

He smirked. *You are paying me.*

Oh, I meant like a psychologist.

I am a psychologist!

She stood. *Want another drink?*

She was an adult with money; she had no use for cheap beer. This round cost double the first, as would the next. He'd made his gesture, and now the tab was on her.

So who's your favorite drummer? she asked, setting down two sepia-toned ryes.

He named a drummer no one respected, the butt of many drummer jokes.

Are you serious? She's awful. I mean everybody knows she's awful.

Joey considered this. *She has no technical skill. But those songs are rockin', and that's accomplished with very few strokes. That's something to strive for, a good beat— privileging that instead of showing off. Simple isn't dumb.*

He took a sip of whiskey and coughed, tried to cover it, gave up on covering it.

He walked her to the train, the air finally cool, then swung his arms out like a pair of rogue cranes. She leaned sloppily into the hug, feeling sad: the night was over, and also male hugs disappointed her. Boys embrace girls with their forearms, hold their bodies back, pull away quick as though she might bite their necks.

> She leaned sloppily into the hug, feeling sad: the night was over, and also male hugs disappointed her.

Want to do this again? she slurred.

Sure, Joey said.

This was a good idea I had, she hollered.

Yeah, he said flatly, *good times.*

So then I'll see you next week then.

Actually I was gonna say. Uh, before. I was gonna say I'm playing a show on Friday and you should come.

Oh yeah?

If you want.

I want! I will!

Cool cool, he said. He told her the venue, the time—it was so late, she'd get home so fucking late—and the ridiculous name of his band, which she already knew and yet still laughed at before realizing she should not, definitely not, have laughed at it.

See you there, she said.

See you, he said.

You go to the show, Mimi said. *You arrive late. You act like you do this all the time. That's sexy. You do not loiter. You congratulate him, then leave. You make yourself the mysterious, sophisticated older woman drinking whiskey in the back.*

I should be breezy, Annie said.

You should be rude, Mimi said.

Yeah, I'm not worrying about some kid.

He's just a penis, a passing amusement.

Annie pretended to laugh.

She arrived two bands into a four-band bill, chin high, making haughty slits of her eyes. She wore a leather jacket, jeans so tight her ass may as well have been picture-framed. She sat at the bar, perpendicular to the stage, which rose a foot off the gritty floor. Red string lights hung limply from the ceiling, and a banner of the bar's logo had been staple-gunned to the wall. Annie ordered the priciest bourbon, watched the bartender's estimation of her scale a few notches. The room was very dark. There were twelve people assembled. The second band finished, and a PA blasted proto alt-rock recorded before Joey was born. She saw him shout into the sound guy's ear, then sit for sound check, executing several stomps and strikes. To warm up he eased into the chill old rap beat he'd taught her—*This is a good beat to play when you want to look cool,* he'd said—then stood to raise the crash, his black T-shirt taut across his back, a suspension bridge spanning his shoulder blades.

Then he tensed as if he'd sensed a predator. In a fluid motion he pivoted, lifted his head, and regarded Annie. He raised a hand. The lights turned him holy, made his arm hairs twigs on a burning bush.

Hey, a slack voice, sugary with rum, said into Annie's ear. Homeboy sidled up beside her. *What's your name again?*

She told him.

Yeah? That's my mother's name.

Neat, Annie said.

Joey saw this exchange—Annie saw him see it—and turned away.

By the way, what's your dog's name? Annie asked.

Shithead, Homeboy said.

She nodded. *They say pets resemble their owners, have you ever heard that?*

He smirked, pulled back—a movement that was entirely neck; he craned it like a movie ninja dodging a bullet—and let his eyes deaden.

So you two, Homeboy said, gesturing toward the stage, *you're hanging out?*

She said nothing.

You think he likes you? He smiled dangerously.

She said more nothing.

Homeboy glanced at the stage. *He's okay, if you're into that sort of thing.*

He cuffed her on the back, took his place beside Joey, lifted a purple guitar, and greeted what could only generously be called *the crowd*.

The first song began. Joey punched the snare once and sat, poised, jaw clamped, stick aloft, tension ratcheting. The reverb whimpered. Annie's ears ached. Joey made a venomous grimace—*a well of aggression*—and licked the snare again, throbbing the kick drum. *Two sounds is all it takes to inaugurate a backbeat*, he'd said: institute an interval, a length between two notes, and you're obligated to iterate it for the duration. *Once the beat's established*, he'd said, *it exists outside of you*. He parted his lips, neck slick; he was furious and precise. The songs were all heartbroken riffs and acidic keyboards, Homeboy's vocals ostentatious and his lyrics laughable. They were not a good band. They were not a terrible band? It didn't matter. What mattered was that it was glorious and horrendous to see Joey play like this after seeing it only in private. What had been hers now had to be shared.

Once the beat exists you're committed, Joey had said. *Even if you drop a stick or something breaks, you can't stop or go back to hit the note you missed. It's gone.*

When the last song ended he lifted water to his lips, a towel to his head, and she waited to see what would happen.

In the story she would tell Mimi, he'd pull the towel from his face and walk off the stage and into her arms—a real hug, a grateful hug, a hug of possession. The show's adrenaline, it seemed, had emboldened him. His shirt would be damp against her cheekbone, and he'd pull back just enough to look down at her and smile sleepily. He'd take her to the back room, his palm on her spine, and they'd find some boys reclined in a weed fog. Homeboy would hand her a joint, and Joey, holding a beer, would decline a hit: *I can't drink and smoke, I get the spins.* He'd tell everybody, *Everybody, this is Annie.* He wouldn't call her his student. And they'd act as though they'd never heard of her, and she'd see on their little faces that they had. Joey would say to her, *It's kinda crowded in here, want to go to the bar?* and they'd go, and stand there folding paper straw covers.

He'd say, *It's awesome you're here, I was watching you, you seemed into it.*

Surely you can tell that I like you, she'd say. *I'm glad,* he'd say.

She'd remember Mimi's advice and say, *I should go in a sec.*

No, Joey would blurt.

No?

He'd say, *I have to pack this shit into my car, but don't leave, okay? Don't leave without me?* And she wouldn't.

The first song began. Joey punched the snare once and sat, poised, jaw clamped, stick aloft, tension ratcheting.

And all of this would be true! All of this would be just how it happened, for real.

And if she were continuing to tell the pure truth, she'd tell Mimi that Joey loaded everything into his car, returned to her at the bar. She said, *Ready?* And this was when he looked at her bemusedly, as though she were someone he'd never met, and when Annie faltered, saying, *Did you want to, like, go back to your . . . to go someplace?* And she'd describe how he put his hands on the greasy bar, stretching out his back like a gym goer, as he said, *Oh, I didn't realize you, I wasn't . . .* and she'd begin to emit sounds, *No no no it's fine, it's fine,* her gut full of helium. In the story Homeboy would come up behind them and sneer, *You guys probably want to be alone,* and Joey, if she were telling the truth, would look afraid and childlike as he said to her,

Well thanks for coming out.

And Homeboy would snicker—a thunderclap, a defibrillator-level blow to her chest—and say to Annie, *Yeah it's probably getting late for you,* and she'd dazedly lay two dollars on the bar, lift her purse, and walk out into the ruins of the evening.

The Manhattan-bound L arrived, and Annie boarded it a penitent wretch. She had brought this misery upon herself. She rode home, where a cat waited and the air smelled dusty and herbal, a merger of century-old hardwood and marijuana. There, she lifted her stack of sheet music, pages of Joey's rickety writing, and placed the papers in the drawer where she kept tax receipts and ticket stubs, greeting cards from her husband.

In one such bar she asked Joey, *Why did you decide to be afraid of me? I'm curious.*

Annie anticipated genuine pain at her next lesson, but knew it'd be dwarfed by the embarrassment, and in the days that followed she'd want to quit, would think up all kinds of ways to abandon Joey: silently disappear, slowly fade out, slap him across the face. She'd tell herself this was a beast that died if starved; all she had to do was not go. But she wouldn't do that, once lesson day came, because she wanted to see him. She'd wonder— why this boy? She'd start with the obvious: grief for her marriage, advancing age. But she'd arrive at the real answer: sometimes you like someone for reasons you can barely name, and that's that, and good fucking luck if they don't feel it too.

It was all so unbelievable. Who'd believe that one day after a lesson she'd impulsively stopped at that crummy but historic old spot on the corner and bought a hot dog though she *never* ate hot dogs? Who would believe that she'd discovered in her internet sleuthing that she and Joey had the same birthday?

Who would believe that she had let this happen to her again?

And who'd believe that she did, in the end, just keep going to her lessons, after all that suffering, his abrupt backing out? Or that they would, in the end, remain friends? That Annie and Joey would belch up beer vapor in various moist bars, talking about their girlfriends and boyfriends, about music, drums, months into the future, long after Annie had found the second man she'd marry. Who'd believe that all she'd have to do to make things cool was go to her next lesson and just play the goddamn drums? The drums!

In one such bar she asked Joey, tipsy but sober enough for it to count, *Why did you decide to be afraid of me? I'm curious.*

Joey had stared at the mirrored wall behind the bar—the mirror in which they could see themselves, actors in a movie and also its audience—a long while before he replied, *This was not a match made in heaven.*

She chuckled. *Because I'm old and lame.*

He turned to her, wounded. *I never thought about your age.*

Then time slowed so much it just about reversed, the room tomb-quiet as he said,

What I thought about, that night and the rest of the time, is how you're an adult and I'm a kid.

A self-contained refutation, a paradox: that he could state this, rouse himself to state this decent and wise thing, proved the statement wrong.

It didn't matter anymore. Still, it was nice to know.

But long before that, her dignity in tatters, Annie had gone to her lesson, the first after that gutting night. She'd walked in and chucked her purse and taken the stool and waited for him to plug in and tune. She didn't look at or speak to him. She lifted her sticks and counted off, then nailed that thorny intro that had bedeviled her: she birthed two flams, the bass drum groaning between each, then belted the crash so hard she numbed her fingers. She remained steady through the measure, executed a dope fill. She committed, and forgot—him and herself, the room, the everything. She played with conviction. She drew from a well of aggression. She let the beat exist outside of her. She stopped asking the drums' permission. She bludgeoned the crash a final time and looked up to find him grinning the grin from before, that grin from back when he was not yet a person, when she hoped to steal something from him, when she wanted his affection so she could throw it away, and he said,

Hey, that was really good.

And Annie said, *Yeah?*

Yeah. You were feeling it. But you kept your wits about you.

Thanks, Joey, she said, calling him, for the first time, his name. 🛡

Brendan Constantine

WHERE DO YOU GET YOUR IDEAS

There's a little shop
at the end of each sentence
where I buy the next one.

In a glossy catalog
delivered every month
from evil.

My ideas come from a cave
my father found in my mother.
It was warm, he said, a fire
already going. On the walls
were paintings of more mothers.

From fire, the word itself, from
everything that could burn us
in the moment of saying it.

Ask me again. Now ask me why
I asked you to ask me.

Really, they just barge in
whenever they feel like it.
I haven't finished a dream
in days.

The first ones came by ship.
Stowaways, they nearly starved.
Then someone found a sack
of almonds and everyone
lived. When they reached port,
they could see in the dark.

From chumps who aren't using them.

From a vending machine
outside the crime museum.

From you. Right now,
you're giving me ideas.
One of them is worth millions.
Another is a small harp
playing in your coat. Still
another is a balcony view
of the parade. There were
supposed to be dancers
in flaming hats. You will
have to imagine them.

From knowing when to stop.
It was a few stanzas ago.

At night, I form a church
with my hands. Inside are
the faces of people I've hurt.
If I want to sleep, I must
look each one in the eye.
I don't make the rules.

DECLARATIVE

I give you
broken

things, so
you won't

ask: *will
this break?*

FIELD TRIP

Today we are going
everywhere in our heads.
To go you must show
your underbelly and a note
from your mother. You
must, on your person (in
your head), carry the
following: everything.
This should include, but
not be limited to: fire,
earth, air, water, snacks
for everyone, and whatever
fundamental elements have
yet to be discovered.
Choose a buddy. Choose
from flora or fauna, from
window or door. Choose
wisely: orderly behavior
will not be tolerated.
Remember: you who
resemble a yellow
school bus: you are
not a representative
of the sun. You
are the sun.

TO THE SUN

Come back
so I
can forgive you.

FICTION

Anvil

Robert Travieso

Annie was manning the espresso machine when Jeremiah walked in. She nodded hello and started the long process of making his cup, a routine he endured begrudgingly every weekday. Anvil at 7:35 with the kids in tow, day care at eight, school at 8:15, first period started at 8:20. Sukey, with her colored pencils and her croissant and her kid-sized whiskey barrel table, would be perfectly content for the twelve or so minutes it took to get his coffee. Deano was asleep, his neck bent unnaturally in the stroller that Jeremiah had had to force over the cobblestone pathway that led to a door just barely wide enough for his oversized wheels to pass through. Sukey rode behind on a little platform attached to the stroller she called her "skateboard," which was convenient and cute, but which made him nervous about her inevitable overconfidence regarding actual skateboarding in the future.

The shop was decorated with the detritus of manual labor, including a small bundle of hay in the corner beside the register, and probably did indeed once have a great big anvil right in the middle of its hardwood floor, as well as a master-forger-type person battering a glowing thing with a hammer, alongside a scrappy Johnny Tremain-style apprentice, who watched and learned and pantomimed in obsequious silence beside him, both in gorgeous leather aprons, the same sort of aprons that the Anvil baristas now wore.

His coffee required perhaps the most pretentious preparation of all, somehow byzantine in its simplicity, essentially a gym sock filled with ground beans and velcroed inside a mason jar, into which just-shy-of-boiling water was poured, in single cc increments, so that his coffee would properly bloom and achieve its perfect blueberry-and-pea-soup balance as he walked the rest of the way to work. If Deano were to wake before the process was complete, the situation would become intolerable and he would have to leave.

While Annie prepared his coffee, he stared with casual intensity at her photo on the wall, as if it might Dorian Gray itself, and she might become healthy again, by magic. Her face, after a decade of anorexia, was what people called "ravaged" by free radicals, but it wasn't really ravaged; she was still very pretty, only now with a kind of Walter Payton mouth guard of hyperpigmentation around her entire mouth, as if she had permanently just finished drinking orange juice from a glass.

They'd ended up together at Hopkins for similar reasons: he because he'd been invited to join the basketball team as a preferred walk-on, she because the track coach had visited her at home every day after school in the spring of her junior year and finagled her a full academic scholarship. And they'd ended up *together* at Hopkins for exactly the same reason: because they were home-sick, and lonely, because they could talk to each other about their respective home-towns, or about the hometowns that had in spirit evaporated for them when they tossed their caps up in the air during grad-uation, and be listened to in earnest. His

> Her face, after a decade of anorexia, was what people called "ravaged" by free radicals.

high school girlfriend had dumped him in de facto fashion during senior week at Dewey Beach, by sharing a joint and making out with a stranger in the ocean while he was in a beach chair reading *Shōgun*. Her boyfriend had gone to Brown and become the all-time leading freshman passer in school history, and then transferred to Cal without telling her. So in the beginning they talked mostly about what they'd left behind, and who had left them.

By her first summer home she was already sick, though he didn't know the full extent of it yet. In the fall of her sophomore year she broke her femur running her sixth no-interval 400 in a row, despite her coach plead-ing with her to take a break: literally pleading, standing there as Annie ran in manic circles around her. They broke up amicably while she was still in her cast, and after that Jeremiah was able to consider Annie's anorexia not his problem anymore, though he'd obviously had a hand in creating it, not to give himself too much credit. And then came a kind of caesura in his existence, a small and not-long-lasting emptiness that he filled as quickly as he could. He'd already been cut by the basketball team, which was humili-ating; the fact that he was six foot seven meant that he had to immediately find a new sport to attach his frame to, if only to fend off strangers, in the way that a beautiful woman must always have a boyfriend. So he tried out for the water polo team, and found he liked it, and grew leaner and stronger and more handsome over the course of the following year. And by the time he saw Gabby Howard charging across the quadrangle in the rain, her knees pumping like pistons, her red scarf trailing behind her, he'd forgotten all about Annie Chamberlin, had almost forgotten she'd ever existed at all.

And in fact by then it was nearly true; she almost didn't exist—she weighed less than ninety pounds. And she was in no condition to compete, not even as a miler, which she'd already starved herself into becoming, but she couldn't stop from running anyway, for miles and miles around campus. This was the only time anyone saw her, and then only barely: a white whippet dashing through the trees in the forest that ringed the quad, running only at night, circling and circling the campus, a pair of shining eyes in the dark, an animal darting through the woods as if powered by a crisis.

> He'd become oddly good at water polo, his floating body a kind of burly mattress that he could rest his own self upon.

She was widely understood to have gone fully crazy by that point, but it got worse. One night after he moved into Gabby's apartment, Annie set up a little cot and blanket outside their door and bivouacked there until the morning. When they stepped outside to start their day, she packed and slunk away so silently that she seemed to dissolve before their eyes. Later she took a stuffed animal he had given her in the early days of their relationship and stitched its decapitated head to their door knocker, its X-ed out eyes facing outward, a curling kind of creepy smile drawn on, like the lion that mocked Jacob Marley.

It was easy enough then to say that she was crazy, and his friends did say that at the time (though Gabby, to her credit, never did). But her actions weren't crazy. They were one) creative and two) interesting, articulate without articulating. *This gift you gave me, which was childish in the first place, now makes me sad in a way I haven't felt since I was an actual child, and so now, in this childlike state that you put me in, I'm so sad I actually need something like this to hug, to make me feel better, so thanks for the perfect gift, only now that you're gone I can't use this anymore, so I chopped your bear's head off and gave it back to you.* Subtextual reference to crazy women with scissors, and male panic, the implied threat of a Lorena Bobbitt, Glenn Close in *Fatal Attraction*: her work—and that's what it was—was strange, but also good. And talking about her work was their path back to a relationship again, to a kind of friendship.

His life was by then suddenly promising in all these unexpected ways. He'd become oddly good at water polo, his floating body a kind of burly mattress that he could rest his own self upon, or ride like a boogie board, as needed, and in the fall of his senior year was named a first team All-American, and transformed into a BMOC in a way he never would have been as a benchwarmer on the basketball team. The other thing that happened was that he'd started writing fiction and in the weeks leading up to graduation had managed to publish two short stories in a well-known literary magazine, with the help of a professor who was friends with the editor.

Meanwhile Annie was sculpting, and painting, and creating performance pieces on the campus green, and making these little spliced-together movies, and showing them in little galleries around town, and making a little name for herself, and going to her classes again. And then she went off to grad school, and when she came back, she was famous—but in the most obscure way possible, famous in a way that seemed specific to Baltimore, where working beside her at Anvil today, for instance, was the guy with the miner's light from Animal Collective, the bassist in Lower Dens, and Amy Reid, who had just put out her first solo album after years of being part of Chiffon.

But she was also still sick, and getting skinnier and skinnier and skinnier every day. He could see it happening in real time, and even the leggings she now wore exclusively sagged at her knees and hung where her calves and especially her butt should have been, the upside-down triangle below her shirt hem revealing the total absence of anything but the balls of her femurs connecting with the sockets of her hip bones.

Deano stirred, and Jeremiah's heart throbbed in response, the same kind of panic he felt when he saw cop car lights in his rearview mirror, and when his child turned and resettled and stuck his thumb back into his mouth, he found himself actually fanning his face with his fingers in order to calm down. Sukey was still engrossed in her penciling, the kids' menu covered with stick figure girls with bob haircuts and A-line dresses. There were bits of croissant all over her face and hands and hair.

Annie handed him his coffee. He could tell by how unpainful the mason jar was in his hand that the coffee would be lukewarm at best by the time he dropped the kids off at day care and walked the rest of the way to school. He asked her what she was working on.

"Actually," she said, "I have a thing upstairs at the Crown. In the quiet room."

"What is it?"

"It's a movie. Another splice job. I did the music too. It's my favorite thing I've ever done. It's called *The Florist*. There's a woman engaged to a banker guy played by Dermot Mulroney, and sometimes Dylan McDermott and sometimes Craig Sheffer. They live in New York, in a new highrise in Lower Manhattan, and their apartment overlooks Brooklyn. The movie opens on the heroine looking down through a telescope at a cute little flower shop in Vinegar Hill. The florist is played by Matthew Goode, and sometimes Blair Underwood. The banker takes her out and asks her to get married in public, and she says yes, but she's pressured, and there's a scene with her alone in the bathroom, splashing water on her face. But she says yes. And so they're engaged, but she has second thoughts, obviously. She hires Matthew Goode to be the florist.

"And as the wedding approaches, she's meeting with the florist more and more, taking trips to Brooklyn, walking over the bridge, and they explore the cobblestone streets together, and Matthew Goode teaches her all about sensuality through the arrangement of wildflowers, and he has these elegantly moth-eaten sweaters, and at some point as Blair Underwood he tells her, he says, 'Maggie, *you* are a wildflower. You're a wildflower. Don't you see?' And they almost kiss, but she pushes him away and runs back to the banker, literally, she literally runs, but she has a wildflower in her hair when she gets back so he's suspicious, and there's this scene where Craig Sheffer bites his own fist for about a minute, but she talks her way out of it, and then it's suddenly the day of their wedding, and she hasn't talked to the florist since they almost kissed, but he's still her florist, because he's a professional, and he's going around putting wildflowers on every table, sort of sloppily scattering chicory and gayfeather and phlox here and there all over the tables, and at first you see it as pouty and mean and passive aggressive, the sloppiness, it's like, come on, be strong, do your job, Matthew Goode, but then the camera pans out and you see it all from above and it takes your breath away, you see what you couldn't see from up close: that he's made a rolling meadow in the banquet hall, a design you can see only from afar, and you're moved, you're legitimately moved, and Maggie's on the balcony now and she's looking down at the tables and she sees it too and she gasps and puts a gloved hand to her mouth, and then *takes off the glove*, and puts her hand to her mouth again and there's a tight shot of her face and her lips.

"And the florist flings open all the windows, in a way that's implied to be against the rules, but what does he care and what does she care about *rules* and the flowers all flutter but stay mostly in place, and the waitstaff clap and you understand that Matthew Goode is not just a florist, he's a fucking sensitive artist who understands things about Maggie that she doesn't even yet have access to herself—but that's what the rest of their life is for, if only, if only.

"Jump-cut to the ceremony. J. Lo is holding hands with the banker, and looking out at the crowd, and her mother is oblivious and crying, and her dad, who knows everything, catches her eye and holds her there and mouths the words *Follow your heart, Maggie,* and he has a single wildflower in his hand, and then the priest turns and asks if anyone knows a reason why they shouldn't be married, and then all these lions storm in and just start *eating* people, just tearing their flesh to shreds. Mulroney, J. Lo, Goode, Meg Ryan, Blair Underwood, the mom, the dad, I put *everybody* in there. There's a shot of Chris Rock just screaming. And there's blood *everywhere*, shattering femurs and tibias, bits of brain and bone, and there's an unrecognizable half-eviscerated body groaning on the floor and the credits roll mid-groan, just slightly faster than normal."

A man asked for a scone and she fetched it. Jeremiah could see Annie's frail chest rising up and down with excitement.

He told her it sounded good, and that he would have to check it out, which meant that he would if he could, which he probably couldn't. She understood. Their lives were running in opposite directions. It was likely meaningful that her body of work was focusing increasingly on a kind of mynah bird patching or pastiche of other pieces of art or schlock shaped to form her voice out of nothing while her own literal body was slowly disappearing, but he found himself too slow-witted or dad-ified to even approach the question of critical analysis. From her barrel Sukey raised her index finger and one eyebrow and was instantly presented with cold milk and a straw in a kiddie cup.

"How about you, Coach?" That's what she called him. "What are you working on?"

He didn't know quite what to say. The truth was that these days when the urge to write came on, he went to the movies. There was also the fact

> He found himself too slow-witted or dad-ified to even approach the question of critical analysis.

that Gabby was pregnant again, and if he was honest with himself he was out of the house more often and for longer durations than was strictly fair, giving himself a little pre-reprieve before the he-couldn't-even-imagine levels of domestic in-the-shit-ness he'd be dealing with come June. Last week, after Gabby and the kids were asleep, he'd gone to the Charles to see all the Indiana Jones films in a row, except for the last one, with the aliens and Shia LaBeouf. There was something ovum-like about that gigantic rock, hurtling toward the hero. The inevitable roundness tumbling down the chute. Had there ever been, and would there ever be, a more famous rock in cinematic history? Maybe the one that landed on James Franco's forearm. Maybe the one that Nigel Terry pulled the sword from, when no one else could. The Ten Commandments. The Hope Diamond. Alcatraz. And the one with Ben Affleck, the meteor "the size of Texas" hurtling toward earth.

> Why did people like what they liked now? *The Walking Dead? Game of Thrones?*

At the Charles there'd been a *coming soon* poster he couldn't get out of his head, a horror movie in which the rooms where various people had been recently murdered were cobbled together into one ultra-murderous mansion, with the ghosts of the murdered people coming along for the ride, and one extremely naive real estate agent on the scene with the keys, trying to rent each room as an efficiency apartment. Or that was what appeared to be happening in the poster art.

Evil ghosts, murderers, witches—horror movies were not really horror movies, in that they didn't really deal with real horror. Watching people get killed or try not to get killed could never be truly horrifying, because the worst that could happen was always death, by evil clown, or evil nun, and death came to everyone. Why had no horror movie been constructed with the plot of a baby in a crib who's been crying for hours, screaming in pain, but the baby monitor has been jiggled and is subtly unplugged so the parents can't hear their baby's cries, and continue reading magazines in bed next to the unplugged baby monitor, making small observations about their articles? Or a mother applies a soothing salve to her baby's bottom after changing her diaper every day, but the salve is somehow corrosive. Or you could just film a baby slowly climbing out of its crib, falling, and breaking its arm, with no one to come scoop it up and take it to the hospital for hours. Or a mother with a boiling pan that topples off the stove onto the baby's face.

Why did people like what they liked now? *The Walking Dead? Game of Thrones?* Where people mostly just got horribly injured? Where men raped women with candelabras, and teenagers got beheaded for sport? Who was clambering for that on a Sunday evening after dinner? The Middle Ages had been brutal, the world was still brutal, but did we need to see the actual disembowelments reenacted on camera? Couldn't someone just come in and say, *He's had it, sir, his face has been ripped off by a pack of starving dogs, it was horrible, but it's all over now*, and then the game of thrones could go on as planned?

What you needed was two people talking to each other on camera, and maybe eating food. That's the movie he would write, if he had the time. And that's what people really wanted in the end, even if they sometimes forgot it, and thought they wanted fully realized fake worlds with the addition of dragons that vaguely mirrored the empires they either came from or that were still controlling them. *People.* That was the thing. *Frankie and Johnny.* Now *there* was a movie. Al Pacino, Nathan Lane, a platonically ideal New York City diner, and a strangely sexy Héctor Elizondo. You watched a movie like that and you wanted to be in love. You wanted to listen to beautiful music with the windows open. You wanted to have a serious conversation. You wanted to have sex and eat ice cream in bed, from the carton with one spoon. And yes they swapped Kathy Bates out for Michelle Pfeiffer when they took it from Broadway to Hollywood, but maybe Hollywood was on to something there. It wouldn't be the same with Kathy Bates. You needed good-looking people on the big screen. Average-looking people couldn't handle that level of close-up.

After they watched it for the first time Gabby had Jeremiah do the thing that Al Pacino does in the movie when the characters finally make love, where he bellows when he comes, signifying the release of all his anger and fear and anxiety in this ecstatic barbaric yawlp of joy and relief and coming, and then they fall asleep, and all the stuff that he shouts isn't inside him anymore. And it worked! Who watched *Game of Thrones* and then wanted to go have sex? Nobody. Or people who got turned on by abuse, or people with very short memories, or people unaffected by art, even bad art—and those were the worst kind of people in the world.

"Hey, Coach?"

"Yes?"

Now Annie would tell him that he was a good writer, and that he owed it to himself to keep writing, etc., things she'd said to him many times before, if only with her eyes, that he had his whole life to keep working on his art, that she was proud of him, and that she would be happy to help him place his work, whenever he had something he wanted to show—

"I think Deano needs to be changed." Her voice suddenly serious. He looked at her. She was frowning. "Like, as soon as possible." Her voice now fretting, her hands flapping with concern.

. . .

In a story, this is where the epiphany would go. Where he would feel how hard the world would be to him hereafter, where his soul would swoon slowly, and where he would discover with a start that he was a part of the performance after all. There was one in every story he taught his students, an epiphany, right before the end, and here he felt his own coming on.

How odd; a part of him was listening to the atomic rumblings of the lower half of Deano, awake now, angry and ready to be changed, straining against his five-point harness, his little one-year-old body knowing by heart or by rhythm how late they were, or how late it suddenly was. And another part of him was watching his sweet, independent Sukey, the dutiful child, lacking in some joy he'd forgot to install along the way. She gathered her pencils, returning them not to Annie, but to the other barista, who was in fact Amy Reid, whose debut album he had listened to in full before falling asleep just the night before, and which had made him cry actual tears of joy, at the music itself, and for the small, strong person who had made it. And now Sukey took her drawing, all those cute askew ladies with their bobs and A-line dresses, and crumpled it up in a perfectly neat ball and tossed it into the trash bin, just as she did every morning. And above it all, in his mind's eye Jeremiah could see, not everything at once, as happened in some of the stories he taught, but just a little ways ahead, culminating in the birth of his third child, who in his vision he now knew would be a boy, warmer than Sukey, and gentler than poor Deano, named Ben, or Bennie, after his water polo coach. And Annie would not get better; she would only get worse; he didn't need a vision to see that was true. She would make her spliced-together movies, crafting schlock into beauty, and continue to struggle, agent-less, to place her pieces in galleries, and nightclubs, and hotel lobbies, in the coffee shop where she worked, and in interesting parts or curated sections of the internet that he was too out of touch to know about, and where very few people would ever see or understand them or care, though those who did would be extremely cool, artists in their own right, and whether you wanted to call that a close-knit community or a circle jerk was up to you, and meanwhile, meanwhile, his own life was growing, and would continue to grow, in both literal and metaphorical fullness, especially with the baby on the way, like a hot air balloon rising up and away from this place. And yes, sometimes it did feel like a great weight instead, a heaviness he could never get out from under, but when that rock fell on that man who was stuck at the bottom of that crevasse for 127 hours, wasn't the thing that gave him the power to start cutting off his own arm with a dull pocketknife the image of his future children smiling down on him, visions from a life he didn't yet have, asking him to please start cutting and make his life continue, so they could live too?

> And Annie would not get better; she would only get worse.

And Annie would get skinnier and skinnier and skinnier, and he would be her witness, every day, until she was too weak to work at Anvil anymore, and for the last month or so of her life she would remain in her little basement apartment on Abel Avenue, eating nothing and drinking only water, too weak to slice a lemon but still engrossed in her work, everything pared down to the essentiality of production, aware of her own impending death and determined to make an interesting movie out of a thousand uninteresting ones, a work gathered from scraps that would go some way toward explaining her time on earth, what she'd seen and felt and understood, and what she still wanted to know, what people would eventually call her opus.

And after her death would come a surprise series of gifts for friends, or GIFs, seven-second ways of saying goodbye, ten or twelve or fifteen of them arriving after her death, glimmers of pure joy or pure anger or pure terror, strung together like pearls, another version of her life's work, made small on purpose, each as small and pointless as her life itself. And he felt that throbbing in his chest again, his heart jumping up to grab him, that cop-in-the-rearview feeling, though Deano had fallen back asleep, and Sukey was waiting patiently on her skateboard. His heart, raging, throbbing with envy. 🏰

Seth Amos

RUMORS OF ELIJAH PHINEAS FLOOD

for Jonathan Nicholson

He would say gods
dwelled in the beams of his barn
and made their beds of his hay,
then he would shoot
a brown comet into the spittoon.
He would say he knew the devil
and saw him every day
in a smoke-gray coat
patrolling the hills at dawn.
He would dance on his porch
like it was the grave of his enemy.
He would sing songs against his hounds
while he pissed on their barbed-wire cage.
He would say the only way
to kill a chicken was to take it to church,
baptize it, then slay it
and bathe in its blood.
He went to church twice a week,
and bathed just as often.
He smoked an ear of corn
still in its husk.
He would drink milk from an udder
he strung up in the corner

of his kitchen, and made sculptures
out of fingernails and mole guts.
He would say the only justice
in the world existed
on his own property.
He twice exorcised demons
from a fence post,
and would say the Holy Ghost
bought the farm down the road,
but wouldn't come over for supper.
He once courted an entire herd of sheep
and would say that God in Heaven
never made a woman so buxom
as a ewe. Once,
he filled his mouth with acorns,
dug his feet into the soil,
and asked God to make him an oak.
Once, the hounds got loose
while he slept and prayed over him
with their hungry teeth.
Once, he woke up in a jacket of smoke
and walked over the hill, out of sight.

DON'T GET WEIRD
a line taken from a conversation with my parents

Don't get weird. Don't lose yourself or forget your appearance, don't walk around muttering soliloquies, or let your daily bread be the prayers of the dead; that's not food on the table. We think it's great that you can recite poems, just don't do it to yourself—we've heard you in your room—don't do it in public, either. We are so proud of you for writing little poems with fine pens on good paper, but let that be it. Isn't paper enough? Then there's the drink, we know the perils of diving headfirst into yourself; you get thirsty. We know you have heroes and that they enjoyed a tipple or two, just don't get weird. Don't drink alone; don't get drunk. If you get lonely, don't turn to women—don't turn to men, either—keep reasonable company. Don't make weird friends. Most of your friends are dead, that's fine. Jesus died (for you). The truth is, we worry about you. You spend most of your time alone with friends you cannot meet. That's fine. Just remember, Jesus came out of his room and he never wrote anything down—well, except for that little bit in the sand, and we're not sure you can call that published. We are just so proud of you, our son, the poet. You don't see many these days. Just out of curiosity, where do you think it will lead you? No matter. You're happy. You are happy, right? We have a hard time telling. Honestly, we just don't know what to do with all of this, but we are so very proud of you. If you ever run out of paper or ink, just let us know.

Sarah Giragosian

THE FOURTH ANNIVERSARY

Bad luck to seed the wedding gown
hydrangea before the green card
arrives, we thought, though we were wedded
four years ago, the first time the law
let us. Last night, light-headed
with wine, our guests spoke of freedom:
how we have it, how others do not,
how lucky to be in this country!
He passed the bird, she passed the salt,
both needing a little bloodshed for paradise,
and in my dreams that night, ICE
burst onto the scene, cattle wagons in tow,
to plaster eviction notices everywhere:
on our doors, our nicked tables,
the sheets on our bed. Snouting the air,
they found us in bed, voided her green card,
drummed Yankee Doodle do or die
into our heads. When we wouldn't sing
along, they deemed us all security risks.
When I woke to the twilight's last gleaming,
I planted my heart under the wedding gown,
the tread of my blackest boots
tamping down the earth.

Reginald Dwayne Betts

A MAN DROPS A COAT ON THE SIDEWALK & ALMOST FALLS INTO THE ARMS OF ANOTHER

as in almost *Madame Cézanne in Red*,
almost falling, almost no longer—as in
almost only bent elbows, almost more
than longing, almost more than unholy,
more than skag, white lady, junk, almost
more than the city eclipsing around them . . .
Winchester gun factory's windows as broken
as the pair refuse to be, the two of them
nodding off of diesel, almost greater
than everything missing, the brown sugar,
the adrenaline slowing them down,
the remnants of a civilization emptied
into their veins. The falling man grasps
at the air. Lost in a trance.
The coat nearly slips from his fingers
as he leans parallel to the concrete,
as his arms reach for something absent.
Whatever about reaping. The men eclipse
the sidewalk & everything else around
them & they sway with a funeral's pace.

These two, their bodies a still-life lovers'
drag. I'm in the car with Nicky & we cannot
stop watching. I imagine one whispers, *I wish
I never touched it*. But who, in the middle
of a high that lets you escape time, utters
such bullshit. One lacks sleeves; the other
throws seven punches into the air
like an aging featherweight. I learned to box
because a desire not to be broken haunted
my dreams. & when Boxer throws six
jabs at a cushion of air, I know once
they both wanted to be something more
than whatever we watching imagine.
A car stops in the street. No hazards.
Just stops. & a photographing arm extends
a camera, offering history as the only help
the two will get: a mechanical witness.
I photo them videoing this world slowed
to 15 rpms, the two men now a movie.
One almost caresses the face of the other.
Lovers are never this gentle, are never this

close to falling & patient enough to know
that there is no getting up from some depths.
A perfect day that's just like doom. Own so
fucking world. They lean into each other
without touching. Horse has slowed down
everything. High like that, you can walk for
hours, & imagine, always, that there is a needle
waiting for your veins. & Nicky says it's a wonder
how something that can have you hold another so
gently could be the ruin of all you might touch.

ESSAY

LOTTERY

Alia Volz

Innocence abroad.

My footfalls echoed in the hushed neighborhood of Batista-era mansions where we foreign students were housed. Expanses of tarry shadow stretched between pools of orange light. A night guard catcalled me from his booth. Oye mami, pa' dónde vas?

Havana felt like a secret world in 2003, an alternate dimension where the United States existed only as a subject for debate. As part of the first group of undergrad exchange students from the US, I had the honor of making first impressions and I took it seriously. Others in my program roamed the city in pale flocks, squawking loudly in English, while I spoke Spanish and made Cuban friends.

Still, it wasn't easy. Not easy to walk down the street, past dozens of underemployed men standing around in the heat, tongues and limbs loose. I'd never been catcalled so irreverently, so incessantly.

I paid the guard no mind, enjoying the cool evening. Rubbery banyan leaves clacked in the breeze like mild applause. Two years prior, I had hiked the 780-kilometer Camino de Santiago, crossing Spain entirely on foot. All along the way, people told me that I should not walk alone.

That I should not travel alone. That I should not, in general, be without a man to protect me from other men. But I was unworried. I believed in a benevolent universe—a capital-U Universe who favored those who asked her to dance. If I made bold decisions, I thought, my life would be momentous and marvelous, and if I made fear-based decisions, nothing interesting would happen, ever.

We'd been in Havana for a month already and I was anxious to see more of the island, so I'd chosen a random town from a map in the steamy bus terminal: San Diego de los Baños, a tiny dot surrounded by a vast swath of green. The opposite of a tourist destination. Buying my ticket in cheap *moneda nacional* meant navigating a complex lottery system, which took two full days, though the ticket only cost the equivalent of two pennies. I had not told anyone in the program that I was leaving for the weekend, lest they interfere; I would just slip away early the next morning. *Jungle,* I thought giddily, *I'm going into the jungle!*

Top 40 pop bounded up the sidewalk from the dilapidated hotel bar the exchange program had rented for the night. It was Valentine's Day, not a big deal in Cuba—no marketing teams cramming hearts down everyone's throats—but the program was throwing a theme party so we could share this tacky custom with our hosts.

During the party, I had learned that my Cuban boyfriend was also dating not one,

Have you already guessed what happens next? Is it that predictable?

but two of the other girls in my program. I felt dumb. Not because I loved him, it was only a crush, but because I'd been hustled. Though who could blame him? He was just looking for a foreigner dumb enough to marry him so he could emigrate. The love con, a classic. For some, it was about money. Others were overeducated and antsy, burning with curiosity about the wide world. My boyfriend was an iconoclast; he yearned to see the US because it was forbidden—which, if I'm honest, was the same impulse that led me to Cuba. Maybe we had more in common than I thought. But that night, half-drunk on bathtub rum, I stormed out of the party to walk home alone.

Have you already guessed what happens next? Is it that predictable?

. . .

When a stranger rode close behind me on a clattering bicycle, that was predictable. When he hissed profanities at my back, that was predictable. When he jumped off his bike and stood over me, tall and muscular and irrevocable as death, that was predictable. When he pinned me to the moist earth between hedges, that was predictable. When I discovered there was no superhero karate kick in my arsenal, that was predictable. When I learned that I did in fact belong to the weaker sex, that was predictable. When I left my body to watch from a safe distance, that was predictable. When I tried to scream and found out I had no voice, that was predictable.

. . .

Before Cuba, I had studied for a year in Ecuador, so my Spanish would be strong by the time I got to the island, so language wouldn't be a barrier. It was at a mall in Quito that I bought the too-tight stretch jeans. I don't know what I was thinking. I guess I liked the color. Pumpkin orange.

Possibly the ugliest item of clothing I have ever owned.

Brother, they were so tight my flesh was like toothpaste in a tube.

So tight that my assailant in Havana couldn't pull them down. He undid the button, but the zipper jammed, and he yanked futilely at the fabric suctioned to my thighs. When he shifted for better leverage, I wriggled sideways and scrambled to my feet. He grabbed my hips and dry humped me standing. Then I was running and running and running and running.

Were the jeans dumb luck? Or was my old pal Universe protecting me?

Perhaps I'd heard the tiniest whisper that day at the mall in Quito: *Buy the pumpkin orange jeans. You never know when you might need them . . .*

. . .

I was no damsel in distress; I was entertainment on a slow night.

The soles of my flats slapped the concrete with a raw steak sound. I ran to Avenida 31, a major artery by which rotting American cars held together with bubble gum chugged into Havana's heart. All the way to the Cupet gas station mini-mart, its illuminated sign a beacon in the night. It was a popular hangout 24/7. Men congregated around outdoor tables, drinking beer bought with US dollars and smoking cheap Cuban cigarettes bought with *moneda nacional*. The dual economy at work everywhere, at all hours.

I stood just beyond the arc of light, panting. What a mess I'd become. Shaking like a chihuahua, mascara streaking my cheeks, snot leaking from my nostrils. Men glanced in my direction. Someone made kissing noises.

I was no damsel in distress; I was entertainment on a slow night.

I retreated into the shadows, afraid to be seen in my weakened condition. Easy prey, wounded gazelle. I could not ask these men for help. I stood in the dark and tried to breathe, while the men argued and laughed about other things.

. . .

Only five blocks to the student house, but what if the rapist was lurking? I could not walk home alone and I could not stay at the gas station and I could not slink back to the party and I could not talk to the men and I could not find any women. And I could not, and I could not. Embassies lined the dark stretch between me and the house—Switzerland, Panama, Belgium—but they were closed, and the night guards often harassed me.

But they were guards, weren't they? Professionals?

I speed-walked, taking a different route than before. At the first embassy I encountered—Switzerland, I think—I paused.

From the shadows came an ordinary catcall—Ssst, mamacita, ven acá.

Help me, I said in Spanish, my voice tremulous. I was attacked just now, right around the corner. Someone tried to rape me.

He was quiet for a moment, and then: What do you want me to do? Go find a policeman.

I could not see his face, but his silhouette shifted in the booth.

Please walk me home, I said. He might still be here.

I can't leave my station.

I'm scared. Please.

I despised this new me with the childish voice, begging not to be a manless woman in the world.

With a perturbed sigh, he called another guard on his walkie-talkie and said there was a panicking female foreigner who needed company. I thought I heard the other guard chuckle.

Wait here, he said to me. My compadre will walk you home.

I felt embarrassed, as if I'd made an outlandish faux pas. I waited beside the booth, saying nothing, for fifteen painfully awkward minutes. The guard who finally came was elderly and fat, and ambled with a pronounced limp. I had to walk extra slow so he could protect me.

When he asked what had happened, and I told him, he didn't seem dismayed. I sensed pleasure, in fact. Schadenfreude. Because I shouldn't have been walking alone. A woman. A tourist. At night. This was what I deserved.

I worried about what this guard and his compadres could do to me if they were in the mood. And the fact that I was afraid amplified the danger. Animals smell fear. Men smell fear.

I no longer wanted the guard to see where I lived. Thank you, I said, this is close enough. But he insisted. I tried pretending I lived in a different house, but he said, No, that's not it. I know where you yanquis live.

. . .

The student house, built shortly before the revolution, was of futuristic sputnik design, all swooping lines and asymmetry. I locked the doors and turned off every light, not wanting to be a silhouette. It was well past two, but my housemates were still out. I bumbled in the dark, stubbed my toe, felt my way along the curved wall to my bedroom, and then locked myself inside.

Psychic collapse performed as if for an audience. The punching of pillows and thighs. The slapping of one's own face. Sobs ricocheting off the tile floor. I felt dislodged from my body. Feeling the sting on my cheek, but also watching from the sidelines with a cocked eyebrow. Literally beside myself.

When I heard my housemates stumble in as one drunken, giggling gaggle, I clamped my mouth shut. From the beginning, I hadn't wanted friends from the States. I'd been aloof and judgmental. Would the girls mask their schadenfreude better than the guard?

. . .

It was three, four, five in the morning. In my hand, a scrap of paper: a ticket for a bus scheduled to leave Havana at seven thirty.

That I would now abandon my bus trip was a given.

If I needed an escort to walk a few familiar blocks, how could I travel solo into a remote part of the island? My fearlessness had been moronic. I was lucky to have escaped uninjured. If I wanted to explore rural Cuba, I'd have to wait and convince someone to go with me, maybe a guy from the program.

Sexual violence was a numbers game, a statistical inevitability; any fool could see that. Move through enough spaces, walk enough streets alone, and you'd be made to regret it.

The Universe had no more power to protect me than a rabbit's foot key chain.

Oh, how I cried over that bus ticket.

When the salmon glow of sunrise leaked around the slat blinds, I smoked the last of my unfiltered Populares. My throat felt like sandpaper, my eyeballs like raisins. I had shakes and chills, maybe a fever coming on. I felt boneless, hollow, innards scooped out like a jack-o'-lantern's. What new self would fill my skin?

Would she still go adventuring on a whim?

Would she slide into easy friendship with strangers?

Would she accept and offer hospitality without suspicion?

Would she charge into the unknown or cling to the familiar?

Well?

I splashed cold water on my face, threw underwear, wallet, and toothbrush into my school backpack, and rushed out the door. Then I was running and running. Not looking at the grassy patch between bushes that I'd smelled so intimately the night before. No time for that. I had half an hour to get across town to the terminal. Thirty minutes to catch up to the woman I had been.

No fucking escort. Just me, my ugly-ass orange jeans, and the unknown.

. . .

The bus was roomy, modern, air-conditioned. Since arriving in Cuba, I had ridden in ancient Buicks, vintage motorcycle sidecars, livestock trailers (with and without animals), and military-style transport trucks. This clean, newish bus seemed extraordinarily luxurious. I took a window seat, curled around my backpack, and before the bus even left the terminal, sank into syrupy sleep.

I awoke with the sensation of entering a dream. The bus ground around tight corners as it climbed through hyper-green jungle. I bumped shoulders with a petite woman now occupying the seat next to mine. Her presence startled me.

Sleep well? she laughed. Though missing a few key teeth, her smile was beautiful, engaging her entire face.

I nodded. My head was pounding. Above the jungle, the sky looked hazy and yellowish, like old aquarium water. We seemed to be floating upward toward some filmy surface.

Where are you heading? she asked.

San Diego de los Baños.

German?

US-American.

She wrinkled her nose. And you're coming to San Diego?

I wanted to get out of the city, I said.

Well, you've made it. She laughed again, brightly, like the high notes on a piano. Our arms brushed and her skin was cool and soft.

Her name was Rita and she'd lived in San Diego her whole life. Her youngest son, seventeen, was studying engineering at the University of Havana. She had visited him in the city, and was now on her way back home. Her eyes filled as she spoke. I miss him already, she said. My sons are all grown up.

She didn't look old enough for grown sons, and I thought she must have had children very young.

> I felt boneless, hollow, innards scooped out like a jack-o'-lantern's. What new self would fill my skin?

Rita asked if I was sick, referencing my puffy eyes and obvious exhaustion.

I hadn't meant to tell anyone about the attack. Now I found myself spilling the details to a near stranger. My Spanish, at this point, was just shy of fluent, and the story rolled easily off my tongue. I amazed myself by speaking calmly, with no drama or emotion, as if the whole thing had happened to someone else. This was, of course, how I would talk about it from that day forward.

Rita listened with a placid expression, neither asking questions nor appearing disinterested. She let me tell the whole story without interruption, perhaps understanding that I needed to say it aloud.

Those things happen, she said when I was done, as if sexual assault were a fact of life. Like getting caught in the rain or dribbling barbecue sauce down your shirt.

And perhaps it is. Just a hiccup in a woman's day.

• • •

We disembarked together beside a treelined park surrounded by stucco homes in pastel shades. It was a pretty town. Not stunning, but simple and nice, with craggy, jungle-heavy mountains rising in the background.

Come, Rita said, I'll take you to a *casa particular*.

I followed her through the park. She wore a yellow terry-cloth romper, a relic from the seventies that would be considered vintage in the States, though in Cuba it was just old. She walked slowly, her movements effortless and graceful. I felt oversized and awkward in my hideous orange jeans, my feet and hands huge compared to hers. My pores gushed rivers of rank sweat, the stench of last night's fear in second bloom.

Rita led me to a two-story colonial, the town's state-authorized *casa particular*, where the few foreigners who ventured here could stay for USD 20. I thanked her and began to climb the stairs, but I couldn't reach the top. My body refused.

Wait, I said, could I maybe stay with you instead? I'll pay you the same. Or more.

My house isn't nice like this, she said. It's not fit for tourists.

I don't care. I can sleep on the floor.

There were things Rita didn't say that must have passed through her mind. It was illegal to house tourists without permission from the state. I was asking her to take a risk. But I think she understood that I needed more than a hotel room.

That's fine, she said, unfolding that wonderful smile again. The boys' room is empty anyway. You can be my kid.

· · ·

> I ate beyond fullness, my belly straining against the orange jeans. Rita kept offering more, and I didn't want to offend, so I ate until my guts throbbed.

I slept on a plank bed surrounded by yellowed family photos and crates of old clothing. I slept forever, through an entire day and night and day, getting up only to pee in the latrine—a rough square cut into the bathroom floor. My nightmares were strange and elaborate. The island of Cuba was a concentration camp. I had been injected with HIV-infected blood and tasked with infecting my mother, my friends, the other women in the camp. Every woman had to be infected. If I didn't carry out this mission, we would all be shot. No lucky numbers in this lottery. My only choice was whether we'd die through swift violence or protracted illness. I still had not decided when I awoke.

· · ·

Dusk. I heard night birds, cicadas, a television. Rich aromas lured me out of bed: stewed meat, pork grease, garlic. It was a modest house with two tiny bedrooms, a central common room, and an outdoor kitchen. Dingy yellow walls, floors of unvarnished wood. Electricity, but no hot water. A faded portrait of young Fidel hung above the sink. Displayed prominently on a shelf atop a doily, a ceramic ballerina figurine in arabesque, one foot broken off at the ankle, the white stump of her leg lifted high.

Rita's elderly mother-in-law sat chain-smoking in front of a black-and-white television with poor reception. Opalescent cataracts cloaked her eyes. Qué bonito, the mother in-law murmured from time to time, smiling at vague shapes of ballet dancers flitting across the snowy screen. Qué bonito. I wondered about the woman's past, felt her history move silently around me. Who had she been before this? Did the old selves inhabit her from time to time?

Our patient's up! boomed Rita's husband, Tony, bursting out of the other bedroom. I'd met him only in passing on the way to the bathroom. He was pudgy, with caramel skin and deep crow's-feet around his eyes, so that he seemed always on the edge of a joke. You sleep a lot, he said.

I apologized, but he waved it off and invited me to sit and chat. My brain felt sluggish. I had to ask him to slow down and repeat things, as if I'd lost fluency in my sleep. Tony told me he worked as a geographer, which I hadn't realized was an actual job. Like most Cubans I'd met, he was well educated, aware of current events, eager to discuss politics. The prior week, John Bolton, George W. Bush's Under Secretary of State for Arms Control and International Security, had delivered a speech adding Cuba to the axis of evil. Cubavisión had aired the speech, and I'd watched it in dismay. How could Cuba—a country without the resources to repair a freaking air conditioner since the Soviet Union's collapse—be considered a serious threat? Tony wanted to know my opinion.

I'm so sorry, I said. I didn't vote for that moron.

All politicians are crazy, he said with an elaborate full-body shrug. They do whatever they want.

. . .

Rita placed a steaming platter of *ropa vieja* on the table, along with a dish of white rice, a bowl of black beans, and a plate of sliced cucumbers and tomatoes.

Rita and Tony sat with me, but didn't eat, and I surmised that they must have had dinner while I was asleep. I was ravenous, and this was the best meal I'd had in Cuba. The meat was obviously local and fresh, unlike the slimy, gristly flesh one ate in the capital. When I'd emptied my plate, Rita spooned out another helping.

I ate beyond fullness, my belly straining against the orange jeans. Rita kept offering more, and I didn't want to offend, so I ate until my guts throbbed, until I could barely swallow. Until the platter was nearly empty.

After I'd finished, I watched in horror as the family ate the rice and beans and scraps of meat that were left.

I had consumed everyone's dinner.

I apologized profusely, explaining my confusion.

Everyone laughed as if it was the most hilarious joke. Especially Tony. He slapped his thighs and laughed until tears streamed down his cheeks. Until he was crying.

. . .

A mug of bland mint tea cooled between my palms. Tony sipped a *corto*.

My woman says you were attacked in Havana, he said. I can't believe it.

He shook his head angrily. He pounded the table with his fist.

That should never have happened, he said. You can't walk around the capital alone. It's dangerous.

But I'm free when I'm alone.

He studied me carefully with keen brown eyes. Then he grinned at Rita. Ésta tiene cojones!

I savored the quick bloom of pride in my chest. *Yes*, I thought, *this girl has balls*. I gave Tony a cocky smirk, and he cracked up. But by the time his laughter had passed, so had the feeling, and I was the new me again, slouching in a wobbly chair. Exhausted.

. . .

Before bed, Rita informed me that I would accompany Tony to a place called La Güira the next day. I gathered that it was some kind of park and that Tony worked there, but the details confused me. What did a professional geographer do at a park? Why did I have to go? I wanted to stay under Rita's gentle watch. But I agreed, thinking that I must be in her way mooning around the house. The dinner incident had been bad enough; I would do whatever they asked.

At sunrise, I followed Tony to a rural road, where we boarded a truck already crowded with men in work boots and grass-stained clothes. I trusted Tony but felt confused and skittish. I did not understand where we were going, or why, or who the other guys were. From the way they eyed me, I gathered that the suspicion was mutual.

The truck wound through several kilometers of hairpin turns. The canopy knitted over our heads, blotting out the sun. We seemed always to be in the middle of an S curve, each turn erasing both the past and the path ahead. I lost all sense of direction, surrounded by an impenetrable chaos of vines, thorn bushes, fierce red flowers.

. . .

We entered the park through a massive stone archway flanked by tall, medieval-style turrets. A mossy stone wall stretched to its vanishing point in both directions. The truck stopped just inside the gate, and everyone piled out. Tony's role, I discovered, was managerial, delegating renovation and maintenance tasks to his grounds keepers. The men broke into smaller teams and dispersed.

Tony gave me a brief tour. La Güira had been the pleasure palace of a powerful lawyer and career politician who'd served as Batista's foreign minister. After the revolution, Castro's government confiscated the 2,500-acre estate and turned it into a national park and *campismo*—a public campground, free to the Cuban people. There were cabins, a disco, two restaurants, game rooms, a lake with canoes, statuary, and a monkey house. The concept of a private party compound being liberated for everyone to enjoy thrilled me. But like so much of Cuba, it had succumbed to decay. Cabins appeared to sink into the ground. Canoes rotted on the shore. The disco, though staffed by a bartender wearing a black vest and bow tie, stood forlornly empty, tinny *reggaetón* playing for no one.

Tony pointed toward nearby foliage. Look, he said, there's the tocororo, our national bird. Hear her sing? Tocororo! Tocororo!

I couldn't pick her song out of the general din, but I saw the bird: small like a sparrow, with blue wings, a red breast, and a white throat. Our mutual national colors.

Tony handed me a crude map and turned me loose. Enjoy the day, he said. If you need anything, head to the disco and they'll find me.

How could I tell him that I didn't want to explore the park alone, that his crew scared me? I nodded dumbly, my brain swimming as I watched Tony join a group of his men. I felt their eyes on me as I turned away. *Just walk*, I thought. *Walk like you're going somewhere, like it's what you want.*

· · ·

I drifted through Japanese gardens. Bonsais gone feral, koi ponds sheathed in algae. The air felt like hot towels clinging to my skin. I wanted to lie down and melt into the grass, but I kept moving, sweat coursing down my spine, and found myself in an ornate, rambling statue garden. Satyr, centaur, mermaid, sphinx. A bronze lion wrestled a giant serpent. A nubile nymph lay belly-down in a slime-choked fountain, gazing up at a giant ram that spat a stream of water on her head.

The jungle encroached from all sides. Vines spiraled up legs, roots widened cracks in the marble. Insects darted from open mouths, ears, eyes. The revolutionary government had wrested this space from the rich, and now the jungle was reclaiming it from them both.

The task of maintaining the park seemed Sisyphean. No matter how diligently the men worked to contain the jungle, it would grow back, intractable as ever. I breathed deeply, trying to inhale that wildness.

I thought, also, about the unruliness of Cuba itself—this tiny island nation whose greatest resource was determination. Despite a half century of economic siege, Cuba refused to conform to the US government's will. This fierce autonomy was what had attracted me. Ironic that my independence would be challenged here, of all places.

A statue of a disrobed maiden stood exposed in a clearing. Perfect peach-sized

> I trusted Tony but felt confused and skittish. I did not understand where we were going, or why, or who the other guys were.

breasts, hair curling around her face, vagina a childish, naked mound. Moss climbed her thighs, coated her arms, darkened her cheeks. My belief in a benevolent Universe had been so naive. No one protected me. I wasn't safe, never had been; no woman was. My unlucky number could come up again and again. Here or in my hometown.

At the edge of the clearing, I spotted a dim path leading into the jungle. The air smelled of chloroform and rot and still water. The old me would have followed that path. So I made the new me try. Just a series of steps: one foot, the other foot. The trail tipped over a ridge and descended sharply into thicker foliage. Shards of hot white sky glittered through banyan leaves the size of my head. Vines draped around me like snakes. I felt swallowed. Through the trees, I heard one of the workers curse and another man answer hotly, some kind of argument. A bubble of terror rose into my throat. I froze, straining to identify their location, to understand their words, but sound moved strangely in that living tunnel. My instincts ordered me to hustle back to the statue garden with its open views.

Then I thought, *This is a test. No kind strangers. No Universe. You are alone and defenseless and endangered by your sex. Now walk.*

One bird trilled louder than the others, maybe a tocororo, maybe not.

I would like to say that walking fixed me. That I became less skittish. But every time I got harassed after that, my skin constricted and my heart jounced. I flinched at rapid movements. Even now, fifteen years later, my breathing gets funky on desolate streets.

That's true and so is this: I didn't stop.

Walking alone. Hitchhiking alone. Thriving in my peculiar way. It's worth it. Only now, there's a private war behind some steps, and some steps are more defiant than others. ⬢

Toi Derricotte

GIFTS FROM THE DEAD

A student said, I've been studying
your line breaks and can't figure out
how they work. I couldn't
explain. All those years they
fought their way to the surface
like cats in a bag. But Lucille
must have given me
breath, because after she died, I
noticed my lines
started to look
a lot like hers! She had told me,
when you lose the flesh
you gain more power. In fact,
that's the only gold
a poet counts on: the power
to give it away. When Ruth Stone
died, she gave me
a new way
to pick up words like those
silver claws in grocery
stores that pick up
stuffed animals and this time they
don't leap away. Ruth had said, just

put your hand
up in the universe and a poem
will jump in. It's crazy
to trust yourself
like that! But now,
I'm learning how
to live.
Even when she was getting chemo
twice a week, Lucille would go
anywhere they asked her—Australia, Alaska—
carrying her thirty-pound purse, which she would never
give up. No matter how we
warned her, she
did it for nothing! On her deathbed, she wouldn't leave
until her daughters promised,
We'll be all right. You can let go.

    Ruthie, starlit, ribboned
and silked, fragile-skinned, like a coat from a Chinese
wardrobe in the Middlebury
Goodwill, told us
she wasn't going to
die. That evening,
after we sank her

down into the hole they had
clawed out that morning,
we sat around the table
where Marcia had planed
the pine slats of her casket
just the day before (her last words,
Marcia said, spoken really
to herself, *Everyone
has to die*) spooning her favorite—
Kozy Shack rice pudding—
right out of the plastic.

TELLY REDUX: SHARON ASKS ME TO SEND A PICTURE OF LITTLE FISHY TELLY

Love is memory lit.

I wish I had
taken his picture but,

in those days, some part of my heart was still
unswimmingly

cold &, as much as I loved

Telly, I couldn't imagine
carrying a fish's

picture in my wallet, or
putting one (in a gold frame)

on the same mahogany
shelf with my grandson. All I have today

is
the Telly in my heart, a shimmery

thinking
in red veils. I remember

his swishy tail, a magisterial emblem

of the Living God. In heaven we will swim together

through clouds & spheres of wonder
far beyond

this unpardoning
glass of water.

from THE YEAR OF BLUE WATER

Robert Hass has a poem named "Fall." It is fall. Today at the
farmers market, I eased my eyes on chili peppers so bright
and gangly and round that I couldn't hold them all. There
were so many. I wondered what they all were holding. In the
poem, Hass's "me" and "you" are picking mushrooms with
a field guide. They get close to the names of things. What
they take from the earth, they try to name in their bodies.
What is it like to eat? The tongue splits for what the tongue
wants—sour rolling on the bitterness of lime, the sweet tang
of tomatoes. Without direction, Taylor gives me a carrot to
eat because they are good and in season right now. The carrot
is wet inside, and sublime.

from THE YEAR OF BLUE WATER

Of all the things I have done, I am most proud of our relationship, of picking up the pieces of investing in each other again and again. I am proud to trust you, despite the pain of trusting that lives in me every day. In every way, I was raised to kill this: the impulse to build and protect a place where you and I can live as ourselves. And not just live. When I hear you on the phone, there's always something else going on, something's happened that will change you or change me, and it's not those moments but ourselves that we share with each other. Not out of necessity, but abundance.

Donald Platt

BLACK PRINCE

Dead brother,
you've become the black prince that Paul Klee painted
on a square foot

of canvas mounted on wood. You're the sovereign of the dead,
black silhouette
of an African prince on a black-brown background so it's almost

impossible to tell
where your body ends and the surrounding night begins. You wear
a crown that is a thicket

of gold thorns. Your eyes burn, jade stones that glow
radioactive green
in the dark. Their half-life is forever. Your nose of pure gold—

a reversed capital L,
sans serif—angles left. Your lips—two horizontal bars, one gold,
one red—are

speechless. You wear a heavy gold collar carved with hieroglyphs
no one can translate.
You're this black-on-black icon I come to pray before. Black prince,

ruler of the full moon
that shines in the upper left corner of Klee's painting like a golden
Russian Easter egg,

we are your people. We all shall walk death's middle kingdom
and bow down
unto you. But on the other side of death's continental

divide,
you were my brother. You had Down syndrome. You put on
a crash helmet

that buckled under your chin and learned to ride a white donkey
named Billy Boy.
The equine therapist led you on Billy Boy by the halter around

a circle of orange traffic
cones in the sandy outdoor arena. She raised a wooden broom handle high
and asked you

to reach up one arm, then the other, stretch as far as you could,
and touch it.
You did. Billy Boy is still alive. You liked to say, "That's right!"

In this life you needed no

other words. Today the sun is shining. "That's right!" I had a bicycle

crash and could

have died. "That's right!" Brother, you died on the eighth

of January.

It snowed. Now it's mid-July, sound of a distant seven-gang lawn mower,

smell of mown grass

borne to me on the west-southwest wind. "That's right!" Brother, be

my black prince,

my mystery, sign of the world I'll never understand.

In your four-fingered

hand, you hold out to me a lemon, a live and golden hand grenade.

Yvonne Amey has an MFA in poetry from the University of Central Florida and teaches college in Florida. Her work has appeared in numerous literary journals.

Seth Amos is co-founder and poetry editor of *Rivet: The Journal of Writing That Risks*. He lives and writes in Brooklyn.

Katie Arnold-Ratliff is the author of the novel *Bright Before Us* and Articles Editor at *O, The Oprah Magazine*. She has recently completed a second novel.

Christian Barter's most recent book is *Bye-Bye Land*. He works on the trail crew at Acadia National Park.

Jo Ann Beard is our hero.

Reginald Dwayne Betts is the author of *Bastards of the Reagan Era*, *A Question of Freedom*, and *Shahid Reads His Own Palm*.

Jericho Brown is the author of *The Tradition*, forthcoming in April.

Laetitia Burns has been writing poetry since age ten. She lives in Los Angeles and is the assistant of a famous Hollywood comedy writer.

Gabrielle Calvocoressi is the author of *Apocalyptic Swing* and *The Last Time I Saw Amelia Earhart*. She teaches at the University of North Carolina at Chapel Hill.

Andrea Cohen's sixth poetry collection, *Nightshade*, will be published next year. Recent books include *Unfathoming* and *Furs Not Mine*.

Brendan Constantine's work has appeared in many of the nation's poetry standards, including *Poem-a-Day* and *Best American Poetry*. He lives in Los Angeles.

Kavita Das writes about the intersection of culture, race, and gender. Her first book is *Poignant Song: The Life and Music of Lakshmi Shankar*.

Toi Derricotte's sixth poetry collection, *I: New and Selected Poems*, is forthcoming. She served on the Academy of American Poets' Board of Chancellors from 2012 to 2017.

John Freeman is the editor of *Freeman's* and the author, most recently, of *Maps*.

Gabriel Fried is the author of two collections of poetry, *The Children Are Reading* and *Making the New Lamb Take*.

Sarah Giragosian is the author of the poetry collection *Queer Fish*, a winner of the American Poetry Journal Book Award.

Rachel Eliza Griffiths is an artist who lives in New York. Her recent collection of poetry is *Lighting the Shadow*.

Aleksandar Hemon is the author of six published titles and has three forthcoming works of nonfiction, *How Did You Get Here?*, *My Parents*, and *This Does Not Belong to You*.

Suji Kwock Kim is the author of *Notes from the Divided Country*, *Private Property*, a multimedia play performed at the Edinburgh Festival Fringe, and *Disorient*.

Alyssa Knickerbocker is a writer and teacher living in a cold beach cottage on the Kitsap Peninsula in Washington state.

Keetje Kuipers' third book, *All Its Charms*, is forthcoming. A former Stegner fellow, her poems have been published in the Pushcart Prize and Best American Poetry anthologies.

Amy Lam is a writer and editor based in Portland, Oregon and Oxford, Mississippi. She is a Kundiman fellow and MFA candidate at Ole Miss.

Maria Lioutaia is completing her MFA at NYU. Her last name means "fierce" in Russian.

Lip Manegio is the author of *We've All Seen Helena* & is just happy to be here.

Airea D. Matthews is the author of *simulacra*, selected by Carl Phillips as the winner of the 2016 Yale Series of Younger Poets.

Thirii Myo Kyaw Myint is the author of *The End of Peril, the End of Enmity, the End of Strive, a Haven* and *Zat Lun*.

Zehra Naqvi is a Pakistani-Canadian writer and poet. She is the winner of *Room* magazine's 2016 Poetry Contest and a 2018 Rhodes Scholar.

Xavier Navarro Aquino was born and raised in Puerto Rico. He's currently a Ph.D. candidate at the University of Nebraska and a Fiction Editor for *Prairie Schooner*.

Donald Platt has published six books of poetry, most recently *Man Praying* and *Tornadoesque*. He teaches in the MFA program at Purdue University.

Robert Travieso lives in Baltimore, with his wife and two children. His stories have appeared in *Tin House*, *One Story*, and *Recommended Reading*, among others.

Mai Der Vang is the author of *Afterland*, 2016 winner of the Walt Whitman Award from the Academy of American Poets.

Alia Volz's first book, *Home Baked: My Mom, Marijuana, and the Stoning of San Francisco*, is forthcoming in 2020.

Tana Wojczuk is a senior nonfiction editor at *Guernica* and the author of a forthcoming biography of Charlotte Cushman.

Yanyi won the 2018 Yale Series of Younger Poets prize, awarded by Carl Phillips, for *The Year of Blue Water* (2019). Find him at yanyiii.com.

C. Dale Young is the author of four collections of poetry and a novel in stories. He practices medicine full-time in San Francisco.

Lily Zhou is a high school senior from the SF Bay Area. Her work appears in *Best New Poets*, *Sixth Finch*, *Waxwing*, *Adroit*, and *NightBlock*.

FRONT COVER:
He Should Have an Umbrella with Him, Photoshop, 50cm x 50cm, 2016
© Seungpyo Hong. www.seungpyohong.com or @seungpyohong on Instagram

CREDITS:
Pages 205–209:"Gifts from the dead" and "Telly redux: Sharon asks me to send a picture of little fishy Telly" from the forthcoming book "I": New and Selected Poems, by Toi Derricotte, ©2019. Reprinted by permission of the University of Pittsburgh Press.

MASTER OF ARTS/MASTER OF FINE ARTS IN
Creative Writing

- Work closely with faculty through workshops and individual mentoring.

- Take advantage of the best features of residential and low-residency programs.

- Choose from specializations in fiction, creative nonfiction and poetry.

- Refine your writing skills in convenient evening courses in Chicago and Evanston.

RECENT AND CONTINUING FACULTY INCLUDE

Chris Abani

Eula Biss

Steve Bogira

Stuart Dybek

Reginald Gibbons

Juan Martinez

Roger Reeves

Christine Sneed

Megan Stielstra

sps.northwestern.edu/cw • 312-503-2579

Northwestern | PROFESSIONAL STUDIES

MFA
CREATIVE WRITING
FICTION – POETRY

TEXAS STATE UNIVERSITY®
The rising STAR of Texas

Our campus overlooks the scenic Hill Country town of San Marcos, part of the Austin Metropolitan Area. With Austin just 30 miles to the north, Texas State students have abundant opportunities to enjoy music, dining, outdoor recreation, and more.

Tim O'Brien
Professor of Creative Writing

Naomi Shihab Nye
Professor of Creative Writing

Karen Russell
Endowed Chair 2018-20

Ada Limón
Spring 2019 Poet-in-Residence

Faculty

Fiction
Doug Dorst
Jennifer duBois
Tom Grimes
Debra Monroe

Poetry
Cyrus Cassells
Roger Jones
Cecily Parks
Kathleen Peirce
Steve Wilson

Visiting Writers*

Kim Barnes
Camille Dungy
Nikky Finney
Rivka Galchen
Ross Gay
Lauren Groff
Terrance Hayes
Marie Howe
Leslie Jamison
Tyehimba Jess
Valeria Luiselli
Viet Nguyen
Nnedi Okorafor
Mary Ruefle
Jim Shepard
Tracy K. Smith
Ocean Vuong

* Recent and upcoming

Adjunct Thesis Faculty

Lee K. Abbott
Catherine Barnett
Rick Bass
Kevin Brockmeier
Jennifer Browne
Ron Carlson
Victoria Chang
Maxine Chernoff
Heather Christle
Monica de la Torre
Natalie Diaz
John Dufresne
Carolyn Forché
Laurie Ann Guerrero
Saskia Hamilton

Amy Hempel
Joanna Klink
Ada Limón
Carole Maso
David McGlynn
Antonya Nelson
Spencer Reece
Alberto Ríos
Elissa Schappell
Chaitali Sen
Bennett Sims
Natalia Sylvester
Brian Turner
Esmé Weijun Wang
Monica Youn

Now offering courses in creative nonfiction.

$70,000 Scholarship:
W. Morgan and Lou Claire Rose Fellowship for an incoming student. Additional scholarships and teaching assistantships available.

Home of *The Porter House Review* and the Clark Fiction Prize

Doug Dorst, MFA Director
Department of English

601 University Drive
San Marcos, TX 78666-4684
512.245.7681

KENYON*review*
WRITERS WORKSHOP

Writers Workshop for Teachers

Literary Nonfiction

Spiritual Writing

Translation

Fiction

Poetry

JUNE 16–22, 2019
JULY 7–13, 2019

To learn more and apply, visit:
KENYONREVIEW.ORG/WRITERS

ABOUT THE COVER

This issue's cover art, *He Should Have an Umbrella with Him*, captures the drama of spring with its bursts of color and torrential rain. The artist, Seungpyo Hong, calls it a companion piece to his illustration *It's Gonna Rain*, which depicts a pink-haired boy in a leather jacket, against a backdrop of water-plump clouds.

Hong studied animation in college, but was also attracted to fine art and fashion design. His training in animation required intensive practice in figure drawing. The form and gestures of Hong's figures reflect that training, as well as his interest in fashion. His figures are stylish, often wearing patterned textiles in chic cuts.

Hong's unique pastel palette incorporates soft gradients and translucencies. He says "choosing colors is the most important and exciting part" of his process. He wants his pastel-driven art to remind viewers of candy and other sweets. His combination of color and facial expressions also lends a surreal feel to his compositions.

Hong prefers to create most of his source materials, in order to ensure that each illustration is entirely his own. He starts with an idea and layout. After a sketch, he takes reference photos or finds existing images of specific elements to draw from.

Hong's illustrations take place in the present; he says he's "not thinking of the past or the future. [His] own feelings can be expressed most finely only at this moment." He makes work about the things he adores and whatever is on his mind. He hopes that when he recalls his work, years from now, it will be "a photo that captures the actual moment of that time."

Seungpyo Hong is based in Seoul and London. You can see more of his art on Instagram @seungpyohong or at www.seungpyohong.com (coming soon).

Written by *Tin House* designer Jakob Vala, based on an interview with the artist.